CLANCY'S LAST WAR

Some crimes are too heinous to go unpunished. Morgan Clancy seeks the man responsible for the deaths of many men, including his younger brother. When the trail leads him to Bluestone Creek, his search for justice becomes entwined with the plight of local farmers and a rancher. Clancy's battle escalates when his meddling uncovers cattle theft, and endangers a young woman, her sister and father. The stakes are lethal and when the final battle comes, Clancy's trail of vengeance may cost all four of them their lives . . .

TERRELL L. BOWERS

◆

CLANCY'S LAST WAR

Complete and Unabridged

LINFORD
Leicester

First published in Great Britain in 2013 by
Robert Hale Limited
London

First Linford Edition
published 2014
by arrangement with
Robert Hale Limited
London

A catalogue record for this book is available
from the British Library.

ISBN 978–1–4448–2174–1

Published by
F. A. Thorpe (Publishing)
Anstey, Leicestershire

Set by Words & Graphics Ltd.
Anstey, Leicestershire
Printed and bound in Great Britain by
T. J. International Ltd., Padstow, Cornwall

This book is printed on acid-free paper

1

Choctaw enjoyed telling everyone he was half Indian and half coyote. He liked to say he had been a scout for wayfaring pilgrims on the Western frontier since the days when the Mormon Trail of '46 had been no more than a deer path. He told stories that no one truly believed about Indian fights, buffalo hunts and cattle drives. At the saloon in town, he concocted tall tales to entertain anyone who would buy him a drink.

He was actually only thirty-eight years old, but he had gray streaks in his hair and beard, more wrinkles than a week-old shirt, and his skin was a sun-parched brown from constant exposure to the elements.

It was his turn to watch the Freeman cattle tonight. They were bunched up in a box canyon where there was feed and a pool of water from last week's rainstorm. Next week, he and the other hands working the ranch would start a drive to Denver. The cattle buyer would meet them there and the worst of the summer would be over.

Choctaw hummed a tune to himself as he rode slowly back and forth across the canyon entrance, glad that the long months of branding steers was behind him. After helping to rope and tie down a hundred head of beef, he had so many aches and pains that he actually felt the fifty or so years-old that people assumed him to be.

He stopped his horse as a shadowy figure appeared in the dark. No one was due to relieve him until sunup, so he put his hand on his pistol and removed the thong so it would be ready for instant use.

'Hey there, Choctaw!' It was a familiar voice, that of one of the top hands for Fulton Armstrong.

'That you, Jocko?' he called back. 'What'n thunderation are you doing out here in the middle of the night?'

Jocko rode closer until he was only a few feet away. 'Gillum said he seen a mountain lion roaming the hills. I wanted to warn you, in case that cat decided to stir up the herd.'

'You didn't have to ride way out here for that,' Choctaw said. 'I've turned a herd of running buffalo with only a stick and a couple of rocks. No way those beef would get stampeded on my watch.'

'Glad to hear it,' Jocko said. 'It'd be a real job to round them up if they spooked.'

'Good of you to come and tell me, but the cattle are all tucked in safely for the night.'

Jocko suddenly drew his gun and pointed it at Choctaw's chest. 'I'm sorry you were the one riding night guard. I never believed half of the stories you tell, but I did like to listen.'

'What's the gun for?'

'I'm taking the herd,' Jocko said, matter-of-factly. 'I've got three hired men ready to move in and lend a hand.'

Choctaw knew he had little chance when he grabbed for his gun. He did manage to get it free of the holster before a white-hot slug passed through his chest.

The bullet caused his horse to jump, but he stayed aboard, trying with his last bit of strength to bring his gun to bear on Jocko.

However, a second bullet knocked him from the saddle and he landed heavily on the ground. He lost his gun in the fall, couldn't catch his breath, and his vision was so skewed he saw only blurred black shadows.

'Rest easy, old-timer,' Jocko muttered. Then he fired again and, for Choctaw, the world ceased to exist.

* * *

Morgan Clancy walked through the infirmary, horrified by the suffering of the many skeletal patients. There were rows of bunks with emaciated, diseased and dying soldiers. These were the last of the poor devils from the prison camp known as Andersonville; mortally afflicted victims who would likely never recover.

'You find him yet?' an orderly inquired.

'His name is on one of the mass graves,' Clancy reported sadly. 'My brother was strong and healthy all of his life. From the date scratched on the cross, it appears he was interned for about five months before he died.'

'Some of these men I'm watching over were in the camp for less than three,' the orderly informed him. 'I doubt a single one will ever see his home again.'

'Soldiers taken prisoner are supposed to be afforded a degree of decency,' Clancy said, his rage barely controlled.

'God must have been looking the other way when Captain Henry Wirz took command of the prison. There's no way he and his ghouls could have been from the same human race as the rest of us.'

'Do you know the final count on the dead?'

'Nearly thirteen thousand,' the orderly replied. 'About one in three of those who were confined in that pit of horrors. And that doesn't include many who will perish from their ill treatment, infections and disease after their release.'

'If they don't track down and hang the lot of those officers and guards, there is no justice in this world.'

'Wirz didn't want to admit how many prisoners were dying in his monthly reports. He claimed he was only interested in making sure none of them ever fought against the Confederacy again.'

Clancy surveyed several men who were missing limbs or were too sick to feed themselves. The gaunt faces looked to have been sketched in charcoal: black holes for eyes, rotted teeth, most were missing hair, having been shaved to get rid of lice. His only real hope was that Jeff had died without too much suffering.

'I don't envy you your job,' Clancy said to the orderly. 'These past months, enduring the smell, the maggots and vermin, the infected wounds and gangrene . . . you and the other orderlies deserve a medal for tending these men.'

'Actually, every man who survived that camp deserves a medal.'

Clancy left the hospital area and journeyed back to headquarters. His had become a familiar face since the end of the war.

Captain Marsh, who was one of the officers designated to process ex-prisoners and stragglers from different outfits, nodded his head in greeting. He had been kind enough to share his quarters with Clancy since his arrival. That had been three weeks ago, and now Clancy's search was ended.

'So you found him.' It was a statement by Marsh.

'I wanted a last look at the few remaining live prisoners first,' Clancy admitted. 'There are thousands of graves at Andersonville, and many bear only a nickname and the number of the unit the dead man was with. A lot of them were buried with no names at all. But I did locate my brother. He was listed at one of the mass graves.'

'We've learned that, at the peak of the over-crowding and starvation, a hundred men were dying each day,' Marsh informed him. 'They couldn't keep up with the records for so many deaths.'

'That's probably why I didn't find his name on the formal register,' Clancy said.

Marsh swore. 'No commander on the battlefield could accept such losses, not day after day, week after week. Yet the wretched butchers who ran Andersonville gleefully watched their fellow men drown in filth and disease. Scurvy, diarrhea, stomach disorders from bad water, malnutrition and untreated wounds — I never knew men could be so unfeeling, so downright evil.'

Clancy sighed his defeat. 'I reckon I'll be leaving tomorrow. I'm responsible for Jeff's death. He only joined the Union army because of me. As our folks had both passed away, he followed my lead, me being the older brother.'

'I'm sorry, Clancy,' Marsh said. 'I was hopeful of a better outcome.'

'The Union took too long to get here, too long to arrange an exchange of prisoners. Jeff was never strong-willed. I'm afraid he didn't have a chance.'

'You've certainly done all you could. It's a shame he didn't make it.'

'I checked every place to which prisoners were transferred from Andersonville first, hoping he was one of the lucky ones. I knew that, once I wound up here, it would be to search for his grave.'

'It was a long and terrible war, Clancy. There's not a single family living in this country who didn't suffer some degree of loss.'

'I guess there's nothing left for me to do but leave it to the war department to round up those responsible for all of the ill-treatment and slaughter of so many good men.'

Marsh stepped closer so his voice would reach only Clancy's ears. 'I'm not supposed to say anything to the survivors,' he whispered. 'But there's speculation that Wirz is the only one of those cruel, black-hearted Rebs who is going to be charged for war crimes against humanity. His trial is to start next month and I suspect he will probably hang before the end of the year.'

'He was the stockade commander for fifteen months,' Clancy summarized. 'Whatever happened, he is the man most responsible for the actions of his men.'

'Yes, but he wasn't the only guilty party. I've learned from the ex-prisoners how some of the guards beat, tortured and even shot Yankee soldiers for sport. There should be dozens of men on the list for war crimes, and many of those should be hanged alongside Wirz.'

'What can we do about it?'

'Nothing,' Marsh said tightly. 'Most of them disappeared, along with the thousands who surrendered. But I did learn something about the sergeant who was in charge of the infirmary. He and several other Rebs made a business out of tending to the sick and dying men.' His voice grew even colder. 'They charged men for treatment. If you couldn't pay, you were left to die in your own misery. Plus, once in the hospital, they robbed the dead and dying of everything they owned, including their gold teeth.'

'How could Wirz let that happen? Didn't the man have any honor or conscience?'

'It's hard to say how much Wirz knew. The sergeant had several guards who worked with him and also a collaborator or two inside the camp. For extra rations and other considerations, the turncoats would secretly point out men who had anything of value. It was a lucrative business for over a year.'

'What happened when the camp closed?' Clancy asked. 'Didn't anyone hold the sergeant responsible for his crimes?'

'From the men I've talked to, the sergeant and his group got nervous when the tide turned for the Union, and the prisoners started being shipped out to other camps. About the time Andersonville was abandoned, the sergeant and several others absconded with all of the loot they'd collected and disappeared.'

'You mean they deserted and got away?'

'As far as anyone knows. There's no record of him or his pals after the surrender.'

Clancy grit his teeth. 'What do you know about him?'

'His name is Sergeant Fuller.'

'Are the authorities looking for him?'

'Everyone in the War Department wants to put the fighting and strife behind them.'

'So they are going to overlook the

fact that up to thirty thousand men were crowded into some twenty-six acres at one time, with no shelter, other than a few sticks, or forced to dig burrows like animals; that the only water for those men was a swamp running through the middle of the camp, which was contaminated with disease and filth? Forget the fact that our boys were given such meager rations, that would not have kept a dog alive?'

'Don't forget the entire camp was surrounded by a dead zone, about twenty feet wide all along the fifteen-foot-high stockade. Step over that line and the Rebel guards would shoot them like rabid dogs.' Marsh did not hide his disgust. 'Such inhumanity toward one's fellow man makes me ashamed for the whole damned human race!'

'And one of the men in charge of the infirmary was robbing men of everything they owned, including their gold teeth!' Clancy exclaimed. 'And that's OK with our War Department!'

'They won't even issue warrants.' Marsh sighed.

'My brother carried our mother's wedding ring on a chain around his neck. It's all we had after she died, back in '61. Pa had been killed during an Indian raid some years earlier. You can bet Sergeant Fuller ended up with it.'

'There's a chance he would have taken the ring. But finding him would be a major chore. Like I told you, he and the others disappeared almost a year ago.'

'Yes, with him running for his life there's no telling where he went.'

'It's the reason I never spoke about him with you before now. I wanted you to focus on the search for your brother.'

Clancy eyed Marsh with suspicion. 'You're holding something back. What is it?'

'Fuller used to get letters from his father,' Marsh informed him. 'One prisoner I talked to had been a medic. He worked inside the dispensary sometimes and saw a couple of the

14

letters. He said the address was from Kansas City, Missouri.'

'All right, but he might have changed his name and gotten rid of the wedding ring by now,' Clancy surmised. 'Do you have a description of the man?'

'Big guy with a lot of mud-colored hair covering his face. He also has a half-moon scar over his left eye and is missing two bottom teeth on the left side. One of the guards who left with him would stand out. He was called Rusty and had red hair, a big red moustache, freckles covering his entire face, a crooked nose and big ears.'

'That's something, I guess.'

'What will you do, Clancy?'

'I'm going to see if I can track down Sergeant Fuller. If the Union won't make him pay for his crimes, I'll see to it he doesn't go unpunished.'

Marsh handed him a sheet of paper. 'This is all I've learned from the prisoners whom I interviewed. That's about all the help I can give you.'

Clancy stuck out his hand. 'I'm going

15

to miss reading from your medical journals every night. I swear, if I spent much more time with you, I'd be looking to attend medical school.'

'Some of those journals contain accounts of the most recent discoveries that have been made in medicine. I wish I'd known some of the facts concerning amputations and the like during the war. It could have saved a lot of lives.'

The two shook hands and Clancy turned to head for the captain's quarters, so that he could gather his few belongings. Marsh called after him.

'If you catch up with Fuller, give him a nice bullet between the eyes for me.'

2

Kate arrived on horseback. She hopped down and hurried over to her father's hired men, Ingersoll and Owens. They were standing over a body that was completely covered with a ground blanket, except for his boots. Kate stopped and put a hand to her mouth to stifle her gasp.

'Choctaw?' She whispered his name, filled with a terrible dread.

'Shot him three times,' Ingersoll told her. 'His gun was out, but he never got off a shot.'

Kate looked up the small canyon. 'What about the cattle?'

'They've been run off,' Owens informed her. 'Looks like they pushed the herd north toward Indian territory.'

'There are plenty of buffalo out on the plains. Why would Indians steal our herd?'

'The rustlers probably took the herd north until they can mix their tracks in with the buffalo. They have enough of a lead on any pursuit for it to be hard for anyone to catch up. I counted several riders and we're down to just the two of us.'

'We lose those beef and we lose the ranch!'

'I'm sorry, Miss Kate,' Owens said. 'But without more help, me and Inger wouldn't have a chance of getting those cattle back.'

'We could ask Armstrong for a couple men,' Ingersoll suggested. 'Four or five of us might be enough.'

'Could it have been Indians?' Kate queried.

'Indians don't usually run off more than the tribe can butcher and eat in a few days. A hundred head . . . that's rustlers,' Owens determined.

'Can you tell for certain how many riders there were?'

He shrugged. 'I've ridden a circle, but it's hard to say. Could have been as few as four, but there might have been six or seven.'

Kate was crestfallen. Even if Armstrong agreed to let three or four of his men accompany her two, they might be outnumbered and outgunned.

'I'll tell Father and see what he wants to do,' she told the two men. 'Can you bring Choctaw back to the ranch house? We'll bury him in the family cemetery.'

'I'm sure he would approve,' Owens said. 'He always claimed that he had no kin left alive.'

'Other than a few coyotes,' Ingersoll mused. 'Remember, that's who raised him from a pup.'

The three of them smiled at the memory. Then Kate climbed aboard her horse and started back to the house. She knew the cattle were lost. Her father would have no choice now but to deal with Armstrong. The idea was repulsive and unsettling. The man had come to the valley and started a ranch next to their own. In a matter of months, he had taken over much of the land they had once occupied. He seemed to have a lot of money and his crew was a curious mix of cowhands and rowdies. He was friendly towards her and her father, but he and his men constantly harangued the farmers.

Kate also disliked the way Armstrong would look at her, as if she were a horse being paraded about before an auction. His glances at her were not provoked by mere attraction, but more from a desire of ownership.

And now we've lost the herd; three years of hard work. We're doomed!

★   ★   ★

Clancy traveled to Kansas City, on the Missouri side, and found work tending bar. Kansas and Missouri had been split in half by the Civil War, and a number of bloody battles had never fully settled the score. Each side clung to its own ideas and there were still a lot of brawls between the two factions.

Most men knew to stay away from the subject of war or slavery, but it didn't stop the hatred. Clancy figured the men he was searching for might feel more at ease among ex-Confederate supporters.

He had hoped to locate Fuller's family, but the only person with that last name, of whose existence he becamse aware, was an old man who had died during the winter from pneumonia. That left Clancy at an unsignposted crossroads, with no direction to follow. With no other options, he decided to stick around for a while and see if he could pick up any information about the elusive Sergeant Fuller.

Destiny came calling late one evening. Two men, both dressed in cowhand garb, entered the saloon and started drinking. Clancy had made a habit of studying and talking to the men who came and went. When he saw that one gent had red hair, a crooked nose and a heavily freckled face, he made an effort to stay close and try to overhear his conversation.

The homely man had the features Clancy had been watching for, but he needed to make certain that this was the right man. Even the mention of Andersonville was enough to get someone killed.

Clancy bided his time until the place had cleared out, leaving only a few patrons. However, when the redhead and his friend got to their feet, he feared he might lose his chance.

'Hey, Rusty!' he called out. 'You're not leaving, are you?'

The man looked like someone had spit down the back of his neck. His eyes grew wide and his bent, ratlike nose twitched. He licked his lips and threw a hard glare at Clancy.

'You talking to me, barkeep?'

'Rusty,' Clancy repeated the name. 'That's what Sergeant Fuller used to call you, isn't it? Come over to the bar and I'll pour you a free drink.'

But no further words were spoken. Rusty drew his gun and fired!

Clancy ducked behind the counter,

as the bullet struck the wall behind him. He grabbed the sawed-off shotgun kept under the bar and rose back up. The second man had scrambled away and men were scurrying in any direction that would keep them out of the field of fire.

'Hold it!' Clancy shouted, trying to stop the man from firing again.

Rusty didn't even hesitate. He attempted to take aim at him and Clancy pulled the trigger of the ten-gauge weapon.

The impact from the shotgun blast drove Rusty halfway out the batwing doors. He sprawled on his back and lay still.

Clancy threw a glance at the man who had been sitting with him, but he had moved to one side and not touched his own gun. To show his peaceful intentions, he raised his hands at once.

'Easy friend,' he said quickly. 'I ain't got no fight with you.'

Clancy hurried round the bar counter, dropped down to one knee and checked on Rusty. It was no use; the buckshot had hit him in the chest. His lifeless body was already turning cold.

'How well did you know this man?' Clancy interrogated Rusty's pal. He rose up from the dead man and returned to the room.

'My name's Kyle Johnson. I'm an out-of-work cowhand from Texas,' the man explained. 'I helped a couple guys deliver their herd to the railroad back at Abilene. Jocko — that's what he said his name was — had sold a small herd of cattle and shipped them from the Kansas City railhead. He bought me a drink and offered me a job on a ranch over Colorado way.'

'You said he just sold some cattle?'

'Sounded on the shady side, because the three men working with him collected their pay and left for parts unknown. He was looking to hire a capable man or two for a more permanent job.'

'He say where in Colorado?'

'Some place called Bluestone Creek.

I never heard of the place, but he said he and his friend had bought a big ranch there and needed some riders.'

'Hand over the gun, bartender.' A cool voice spoke up from behind Clancy.

One of the local lawmen had entered. His own gun out, in case Clancy decided to challenge his right to disarm him. Without questioning the cowhand further, Clancy handed his shotgun to the deputy.

* * *

Kate Freeman was in the next room, a few feet from where her father and the new rancher were in serious conversation. Her teeth were clenched; her jaw was locked in dread and apprehension as she listened to the two men.

Thomas Freeman had never fully recovered from being tossed from a horse shortly after his sixtieth birthday. He was still too feeble to walk more than a few steps at a time. Presently he was seated in the comfortable padded chair in the sitting room. Fulton Armstrong remained standing; he was a man who seemed to enjoy using any advantage at hand.

'We have agreed on the price and conditions of this partnership,' Armstrong outlined. 'You have only to sign the contract and have it witnessed.'

'I'm not eager to lose control of my ranch,' Thomas replied.

'You will lose it altogether if I don't pitch in and make your mortgage payment,' Armstrong reminded him curtly.

'I still have enough cattle to make it,' Thomas said.

'Only if you sell every beef on the place. You'll be broke.'

Tom squirmed uncomfortably. 'You can't blame me for wanting a little time to consider this decision.'

'You need a strong partner to save the ranch,' Armstrong stated unequivocally. 'The growth in the valley is threatening the flow of water for the cattle. The farmers will steal the water to irrigate their fields next season. I'm afraid, during the heat of summer, the creek will be dry before it reaches the western pastures.'

'There's only a handful of hard-working farmers, Fulton. I lost my sons at Gettysburg, but I harbor no ill will against them. As for the irrigation, I'm certain they won't use so much water as to dry up the stream.'

'If you're not worried about them, I'll agree to let them stay,' Armstrong assured the old man. 'And my own house is nearly built, so you can continue to live here for the remainder of your days. What have I left undone?'

'My daughters,' Thomas replied. 'Having lost both of my sons in the war, I need to know they will be well cared for.'

'The marriage between your daughter and me takes care of that.'

'Yes, but what about Jenny?'

Kate leaned forward slightly, her ears straining to hear the next words. Jenny was not a normal girl of sixteen. Her body had grown with the years, but her mind remained that of a child.

'There is a special asylum for . . . unfortunates, in Denver,' Armstrong suggested. 'I'm sure she would be well taken care of there.'

'Bah!' Thomas snorted his contempt. 'An alms house, madhouse, a house for the insane! Jenny is not crazy or dangerous, she's a child.'

'Perhaps,' Armstrong allowed. 'But what future is there for her? She is a six-year-old in a body that will age physically until she is old and withered. What kind of life can she have here?'

'She can be loved like one of the family,' Thomas stated firmly. 'She does her chores, keeps her room tidy, and is loving and sweet.'

'You expect me to take her like I would a child?' Armstrong's tone of voice revealed his revulsion at the idea.

'She would be your sister-in-law,' Thomas maintained. 'And let's not forget, you are twice the age of Kate.

Even if you stay in good health, she will likely be a widow in fifteen to twenty years. She would look after Jenny after you're gone.'

There came a long silence in the room. Kate held her breath, alert for Fulton Armstrong's reply. After a time she heard the large man sigh.

'I accept your terms, Tom,' he acquiesced. 'Jenny can live here with you, until you can no longer care for her. Then she will be welcome to move in with us.'

The relief was plain in her father's voice. 'Thank you, Fulton. We can make the announcement to everyone at the Sunday meeting. What do you think, four or five months for the engagement and a spring wedding?'

'I'm more in favor of making a wedding announcement,' the other man countered. 'Let's make it the first of next month. We'll get it out of the way before winter sets in.' Before Thomas could offer up an argument, he added: 'And we can sign the contract papers the very same day. No need to put either chore off any longer than that.'

Marrying me is a chore, something to get out of the way! Kate seethed silently. What unmitigated gall! Fulton Armstrong was a pompous, arrogant, land-grabber, with not the slightest bit of integrity. She wouldn't be a wife to him, she would be his property, a parts deal to win control of her family's ranch.

Kate slipped off to her room, threw herself on to her bed and sobbed into her pillow. She had put off suitors and admirers for years, mostly for the sake of Jenny. She had made it clear to any man who showed an interest in courting her that she would not abandon her little sister. Unfortunately, that condition had driven a number of men away. It was hard enough to start a life as a couple, without having an extra child around. Plus, Jenny would always be a part of the family, and she might never be older than eight or nine mentally.

Her worry and concern for her sister had doomed her to a marriage with Fulton Armstrong, a man who had come to the valley searching for his fortune. With a goodly amount of money, and building his ranch a mere mile away, he had weaseled himself into her father's confidence and forged a partnership. It had been a calculated move to take over the Freeman ranch and it had worked. With her father's ailing health, and the loss of the hundred steers which would have strengthened the ranch, Thomas had given in. He had let the man into their lives and now Armstrong was going to dictate over their ranch . . . and the rest of her life!

★ ★ ★

The judge and the US marshal sat across from Clancy. There had been no charges brought against him, in view of the obvious self-defence shooting of the man in the saloon. This conversation was more about why the shooting had occurred.

'So you believe this Rusty character was one of the guards from Andersonville?' asked the judge. Even though these two men had supported the Confederacy, no man with a decent bone in his body condoned the heinous treatment of prisoners in that hellhole.

'He fit the description, and he tried to kill me when I called him by name,' Clancy replied.

'What about the cattle he sold? What happened to the money?' the judge asked the marshal.

'According to the manager over at the Cattleman's Bank, Jocko deposited the funds into the account of a man named Fulton Armstrong.'

'What's your take on that?' the judge queried.

'The cattle were marked with a new brand, one that was filed about six months ago. It belongs to a new ranch, over in Colorado, calling itself the Diamond T.' He added curiously,

32

'There is already a Big Diamond ranch, so the brands would be easy to combine.'

'And this man you're looking for, this Sergeant Fuller,' the judge now looked at Clancy, 'you think he might be this man in Colorado?'

'It's possible,' Clancy said.

'And you're certain this Fuller is the one from Andersonville, responsible for a host of crimes against humanity?' the marshal inquired.

Clancy dug out the deposition that Captain Marsh had given him. He handed it to the judge so he could read it. As the judge glanced over the paper Clancy explained the wording to the marshal.

'Fuller caused the deaths of an untold number of soldiers. He charged them a fee for medical aid; those who couldn't pay perished. He also robbed the dead bodies of anything of value, including their gold teeth.'

'Why isn't the army after this man?' the judge wanted to know.

'Because President Johnson and the men in power want to put the war behind them. You can't heal a country if you keep fighting a war that has ended. They grabbed Captain Wirz so that they could make an example out of him. He will likely be hanged for his part in the crimes commited at the prison camp. But his trial and punishment is mostly to appease the public sentiment.'

'With no warrant out for this Sergeant Fuller, how do you intend to deal with him?' the marshal asked.

'If I get him to admit who he is, and I can find out what happened to my mother's ring — the one my brother wore around his neck — I'll settle accounts for a few of the thirteen thousand men who died in Andersonville.'

'You're talking murder,' the judge said, handing back the paper.

Clancy put away Marsh's letter and laughed without mirth. 'A man like him? He won't want me telling anyone who he is. 'Most everyone in the country has heard about the horrors in Andersonville. He'll have to kill me to shut me up.'

The marshal queried: 'If this man owns a ranch, he will likely have a few hired men working for him. How are you going to handle that?'

'Rusty told the cowhand that their ranch was over at a place called Bluestone Creek and that they needed help. I can hire on to work cattle until I find out if he's the man I'm looking for.'

'We have an office in Denver,' the marshal said. 'Let me do a little checking before you go off on your vendetta. War crimes aside, if he was robbing dead men of the gold in their teeth and other valuable possessions, I'm sure we can find something to charge him with.'

'I told Hal, at the saloon, that I would work till the end of the week. I need the wages for traveling money.'

'I'll get back to you on this,' the marshal said. 'Give the judge and me a little time; maybe we can figure a way to do this legal. It shouldn't take more than a day or two.'

'Like I said, I'll be here till the end of the week.'

3

Ringer came over to stand next to Armstrong. The two of them watched as Jenny pulled a toy wagon across the yard. She was giving her favorite doll a ride.

'So she's going to be part of the family.' Ringer snickered. 'Bet you're looking forward to having her around. You'll look real good with her sitting on your knee.'

'She's sixteen, Ringer,' Armstrong quipped back. 'In a couple of years, you can take her for your wife. Problem solved.'

Ringer laughed at the idea. 'I once heard a word to describe a man who liked little girls in the wrong way, boss. Ain't no one ever going to call me that.'

'What the hell am I gonna do with a woman-sized child?' Armstrong grumbled. 'I didn't mind the idea of marrying Kate.

She's not the most beautiful woman I've ever seen, but she's passable.'

'More than passable,' Ringer countered. 'I sure wouldn't toss her out of the house for burning my toast.'

'Yes, but she is a part of the deal — got to take both her and her sister.'

'Maybe we can trade Jenny to the Indians.' Ringer grinned. 'They would probably only want a dozen horses to take her off of your hands.'

'What's going on with the farmers?' Armstrong changed the topic.

'We've been doing like you said. Flint and Cole ran some cattle through some of their fields a few nights back. Wart bullied a couple of the men down by the creek and Arno shot a milk cow. We've got them scared to go anywhere alone.'

'I told Freeman I would let them stay, but let's keep up the pressure. Have the boys make it war related, as if we are all ex-Yankees. With the farmers being from Missouri, it will look like a feud between us and a bunch of Rebels.

That way, there won't be any lawman coming along and taking their side.'

'Nearly every man who served in the war has come home, boss. You really think there's a chance someone will show up who can recognize you?'

'It's a long shot, but it doesn't hurt to be careful. One of them might have a relative visit, or invite some of their farmer friends to move here. It would only take one person who knew me to ruin everything.'

'You're the boss.'

'Once we have control of Freeman's ranch, we will be too big to mess with. For the time being, we need the bulk of the people in town to support us on this issue. We want them on our side.'

'Hank Vogel and Len Silva are the only two who carry weight, being that they own the general store and saloon. They are Union supporters and, with the money we've brought to this town, both of them should back whatever we do.'

'What about the feisty old wart who

runs the livery and stage office?'

'York's like a puff of hot air with no wind, boss. Him and Granny won't give us any trouble.'

'They might side with the farmers.'

'If they do, we'll make them regret it.'

'All right, Ringer. Tell the business owners to keep a sharp eye for anyone who looks to be bringing trouble our way. We can't let anything stop us from gaining control of Freeman's ranch.'

'There ought to be a lesson taught today, boss. Gillum and Quint are going to town this morning.' Ringer snickered. 'They are going to make a nuisance of themselves when the Baker family arrives to buy their monthly supplies.'

Armstrong grinned. 'Mighty neighborly of our boys to check up on the Bakers. Stony is the unspoken leader of the farmers. If he caves in, the others will follow.'

'I'll inform the boys to pass along a friendly word of warning to the businesses while they are in town.'

Armstrong gave an affirmative bob of his head. 'I'll see you later.'

Ringer left him and headed off to find and give instructions to the two ruffian cowhands. Armstrong's attention went back to Jenny. She was still in the yard, and now had Shakes, the family dog riding in the wagon. She giggled when Shakes became nervous about her erratic driving and jumped out of the wagon. It was a child's laughter, sounding a bit strange coming from a slightly chubby, sixteen-year-old girl.

Armstrong grimaced at the idea of having Jenny live in his house for the remainder of his life. With a young and healthy wife like Kate, he expected to have two or three children of his own. He wasn't keen on the idea of having a sister-in-law who would always remain a child. With a wicked twist of his lips, he made a decision.

Soon as the old man dies, I'll ship her to an asylum in Denver and to hell with what Kate wants!

41

Darren Baker was in trouble. The two riders from the Diamond T — he knew them as Gillum and Quint — had approached as soon as he finished loading the store-bought goods in the back of the wagon. The farmers had never had a problem with Thomas Freeman. But Fulton Armstrong had pretty much taken over Tom's ranch. He had it in for anyone who had fought for or supported the Confederacy. At nineteen years of age, and the oldest child of the family, Darren was young enough not to have had to serve in the war. He had stayed with his family when they moved from Missouri and helped start their new farm along the Bluestone Creek bottomlands. He had learned a lot about farming, but very little about fighting.

'We're here to help with your supplies, farmer boy,' Gillum sneered, moving between him and the wagon.

'That's right, Johnny Reb.' Quint

joined in with the razzing. 'Hate to see your poor horses work so hard pulling all that weight.'

'We ain't Confederates,' Darren replied. 'No one in our family fought on either side during the war.'

'Must be a family of cowards,' Gillum stated. 'They're a bunch of yella-dog cowards, Quint.'

'Come on, guys,' Darren attempted to brush off the heckling. 'I've got to get started for home.'

Gillum was a full head taller than Darren. He stepped forward, forcing Darren to back up a step. The man's look betrayed his purpose and it sent shivers up Darren's spine.

'You ain't got no home, coward,' Gillum said thickly. He paused to spit a stream of tobacco juice, most of it landing on the toe of Darren's boot. 'You and them other farmers are stinkin' up the whole valley. It's time you were moving on.'

'I don't want any trouble,' Darren said, hating the weakness in both his voice and his knees. 'Come on, Gillum. Let me get going.'

Gillum's lips curled upwards, baring his tobacco-stained teeth. 'Oh, I'm gonna let you go . . . to hell!'

Darren should have been prepared. Had he ever been in a fistfight before, he would have known to duck, to cover up with his arms to protect himself. But the knuckles from Gillum's fist blasted him full in the face. The force knocked him back two steps, where he was tripped by Quint. He landed flat on his back in the middle of the street.

Raucous laughter rang in his ears, while he suffered a blinding numbness from being struck. He attempted to rise, pulling his legs under him. But a heavy boot struck him in the jaw. He was barely clinging to consciousness when a second foot kicked him in the ribs. Darren curled up in a fetal position, arms over his face for protection, fearful he was going to be kicked to death.

★ ★ ★

Morgan Clancy was in the store, picking up a few necessities. He had intended to quiz the store-keeper about the rancher, Fulton Armstrong, when the fight broke out. He glanced out of the window to see the boy being knocked to the ground. Placing his items on the counter to be tallied for payment, he asked: 'What's the beating all about?'

'The kid is a farmer,' the man replied. 'Most of the farmers here came from Missouri, but accusing him of being a Confederate is only an excuse. Fulton Armstrong wants the valley and water for his cattle. Gillum, the taller man, and Quint are a couple of his men.'

'Any law in town?' he asked quickly.

'Nope,' the storekeeper replied. 'The US marshal comes by on occasion, but that's all we got.'

When the two men began to kick the boy, Clancy decided to take a hand. He charged out of the door and slammed Gillum with his shoulder, driving him into Quint. Both of them were knocked off their feet and tumbled into the thick dust by the hitching post.

'I believe the kid's had enough,' Clancy told them.

Gillum was the first to get to his feet. He brushed himself off and sized up the newcomer.

'Who do you think you are?' he demanded to know.

'Name's Clancy.'

Quint was standing now too, both men facing Clancy. Quint gave him a wicked look. 'You a Reb sympathizer or something?'

'Not me. I fought for the Union.'

'Well, hey, Clancy,' Quint said amiably. 'We're ex-Yanks too. You're sticking up for the wrong side here.'

'The war's over,' Clancy replied. 'It's been over for several months.' Then he tipped his head at the semi-conscious boy on the ground. 'Besides that, the kid looks a mite too young to have been wearing a uniform and fighting for the South.'

'His family moved here from Reb country,' Gillum said. 'That's enough for us.'

Clancy was unmoved. 'The war is over,' he repeated firmly. 'And you've made your point.'

Quint snorted his disgust. 'I got an idea you didn't fight with us Yankees. There ain't anyone else around here sticking their neck out for this Rebel scum.'

'Man's got a real poor sense of loyalty,' Gillum joined in. 'Maybe we ought to teach him a lesson too?'

Clancy put his hand on the butt of his LeMat revolver. He knew he couldn't take on the two toughs with his fists and expect to remain in one piece.

'Let's keep our heads, boys,' he warned. 'You've no call to pull iron on me.'

Gillum guffawed. 'Hear that, Quint?' He backed up a step and lowered his hand to his own pistol. 'He thinks he can buffalo the two of us!'

Quint didn't reply in words; he

grabbed for his gun.

Clancy jerked the .42 caliber revolver and fired in the same motion. His aim was true. The bullet tore through Quint's chest and he staggered sideways. His bumping into Gillum was enough to ruin the man's draw. By the time Gillum could get his gun free and adjust his aim, a second round from Clancy's gun hit him in the chest as well.

Clancy held his fire as both men went down from their injuries. He moved in and kicked their pistols out of reach, but it was an unnecessary precaution. Gillum's eyes were already open and fixed, staring at the sky blindly. As for Quint, he groaned and tried to roll over, but didn't quite manage the feat. He ceased breathing and lay with his body grotesquely twisted and his face in the dirt.

The storekeeper came out and looked at the two bodies. 'You sure made an impression on your first day in town, stranger. What kind of work did you say you were looking for?'

Rather than answer him, Clancy knelt over the dazed young Darren and helped him to sit up. He was bleeding some from his nose, and one eye was nearly closed from the swelling. After Clancy had checked him over, the youngster could take a deep breath without wincing and nothing appeared to be broken.

'Why did you stick up for me?' the boy asked. He looked through his one good eye. 'Didn't I hear you say that you fought with the Yankees?'

'Like I tried to tell those two bullies, the war is over. We've had enough fighting and killing.'

The kid dabbed at the blood to stop it from running from his nose. 'Yeah,' he said cynically, looking at the two dead ranch hands. 'I can see you're a man of peace and good will.'

As the boy appeared sound enough to look after himself, Clancy stood up and faced the storekeeper.

'This town have a telegraph?'

'At the stage office over yonder.' The storekeeper gestured to the livery stable. 'Frosty York and an old maid relation of his handle the post, stage, blacksmithing . . . you name it.'

'I'll be back and pick up the items I left on your counter. First, I need help to tend to these bodies.'

'That'd be York too. He's the undertaker and tends to the graveyard.'

Clancy turned to the farmer boy. 'Help me get these two men moved out of the street. Then I'll go over and talk to this Jack of all trades — Frosty York.'

★   ★   ★

Granny came out of the office and stopped at York's side.

'I thought I heard shooting,' she said.

'Looks like business for us.' He turned and hurried into the combination barn, shed and blacksmith shop.

'We could use a paying customer,' Granny announced, having followed him. 'I need to buy flour and sugar.'

'I'm working on a wagon for Armstrong. Soon as I finish the repair, we'll have a couple dollars for that.'

The woman sighed. 'You and I manage a dozen jobs between us and still we never have an extra dime.'

'It's still better than living off your sister, ain't it?' he asked. 'I mean, you have the stage, the telegraph and the mail. It's a regular job and you do for yourself.'

A rare smile came to the woman's lips. 'Yes, Frosty. It was good of you to ask me to move here. I'm sure Zelda appreciates it too.'

He picked up a hammer. 'If you run short of money, take a little out of the box.'

'That's your retirement money. You can't go dipping into that.'

'I'll probably work till the day I die,' he said matter-of-factly. 'If we run out of something, go ahead and take what we need.'

'Thank you, Frosty.' Granny's voice was sincere, but she added with a little dry humor, 'However, I think I'll put off shopping until the dead bodies are off the street.'

'Like I said, it looks like business for me.'

* * *

Clancy reached the livery and saw that a man had pulled one wooden box over to stand near the door and was hurriedly pounding nails to finish off a second. A medium-height man, muscularly built, with white hair and a hawklike squint, York wasn't wearing a hat, but had on a heavy work-apron. He paused from his chore and offered up a crooked grin.

'Two dollars each for the box,' he greeted Clancy. 'Another two each if you want me to bury them polecats. I'll stick up a wooden cross for nothing, but a marker with names and dates will cost another dollar each.'

'You must be Frosty York,' Clancy said.

'In the flesh.'

'Well, payment for the burial for those two men is something you'll need to hash out with whoever claims the bodies. I'm more interested in sending a telegraph message to the US marshal's office in Denver. I'd prefer not to have a wanted poster with my face on it.'

'Being that those were Fulton Armstrong's boys, you don't have to worry about ending up on a wanted notice. You'll likely be pushing up dirt with your snoot before the ink has time to dry on the paper.'

'You're saying the man might take exception to my actions?'

York chuckled. 'He once horse-whipped a man who bumped into him and caused him to spill his drink at the saloon.'

'Sounds like a man to step aside for.'

'He don't scare me none, but I got nothing to lose but my life.' York regarded him thoughtfully. 'How much have you got to lose?'

'How about that telegram?' Clancy asked, showing some impatience.

'Granny is inside. She manages the office most of the time.'

'Granny?' Clancy frowned. 'If she's your grandmother, she must have been around when Moses was a child.'

York gave a shake of his head. 'She ain't my granny,' he explained. 'She is actually my sister-in-law's spinster sister. She lived with my brother and his wife until he died a few years back. It's been hard times since the war and my brother didn't leave much money behind. My sister moved in with one of her kids, but Granny needed a job. I told her I could use the help, so we share a house and this here business. Her first name was Grainne. She preferred Granny.' He eyed Clancy with a challenge, as if he might say something about a man and a woman sharing the same house when not blood-related. Clancy waited patiently until York puffed up his chest and asked: 'Any more questions?'

'No chance of that. If it took you that much wind to answer a second question,' Clancy teased, 'it would be faster for me to ride over to Denver and tell the marshal in person what happened.'

'All right, sonny.' York snorted. 'I told you about Armstrong riding roughshod over the whole valley. My conscience is clear. You can get yourself kilt now and I won't have no regrets. I warned you to mount your hoss and to put his nose into the wind.'

'That's right neighborly of you, but I've got some business hereabouts. I won't be leaving until I've finished.'

While York started work on the second coffin Clancy went into the office. It was cluttered with some boxes on one side, but there was a counter in the front. Along the wall were several shelves, sectioned off with a dozen or so compartments for sorting mail. On a desk at the counter was a telegraph key and note pad.

Clancy was about to call out to see

where the Granny person was when she came from a back room. About the same age as Frosty York, she had gray hair tied back in a bun, and wore a dark-brown work dress that had seen better days.

'I thought I heard someone talking to Frosty,' she said in greeting. 'What can I do for you, young man?'

'I'd like to send a telegram.'

'You're new in town.' It was a statement. 'Were you involved in the shooting?'

'Uh, yes,' Clancy said. 'It's why I need to send a telegram.'

'Write down what you want me to say while I get the line open,' she said, straddling a stool next to the counter. 'It's two bits a word, so you might want to keep the message short and to the point.'

Clancy took the offered pencil and scribbled the note. Granny quickly got through to the Denver office and transmitted the message. Then she frowned up at Clancy.

'You didn't ask for a reply.'

'No, I didn't.'

'You told the marshal that you killed two men while defending a farmer?'

'That's right.' Clancy said.

'When I said to keep the message short, you took it to heart,' Granny remarked. 'What makes you think that them what's lawful-minded won't figure you ought to be questioned by a judge?'

'You don't have a judge in Bluestone Creek, do you?'

'No,' Granny admitted. 'But that doesn't mean someone isn't going to want you to explain the deaths of two men.'

'I did explain it.'

Granny's expression was one of disbelief. 'Mister, if I was you, I don't think I'd take up lawyering. You don't have the gift of gab needed for the job!'

Clancy paid for the telegraph message. Before leaving he said, 'I reckon I ought to talk to the boss of the two men I was forced to shoot. That way, he will know to get in touch with your partner as to the burial details.'

'I wash my hands when it comes to helping someone commit suicide. You better speak to Frosty about such an unhealthy notion.'

Clancy returned to where York was finishing up his carpentry. 'Good,' he said. 'You're just in time to help me cart those two bodies over here for a final fitting.'

'I'll lend a hand, but then I'd like directions to Armstrong's ranch. I need to tell him about his two hired men.'

The older man gawked at him as if thinking the stairway to his brain was missing a few steps.

Clancy ignored him long enough to replace the two spent rounds with .42 caliber cartridges. Seeing the gun caused York to squint in puzzlement.

'That there shooting iron holds more bullets than any revolver I ever seen before,' he said. 'And what's the second barrel for?'

'The LeMat carries nine cartridges, plus a single 20-gauge round of buckshot. Some call it the grapeshot revolver.'

'I've heard tell of such a gun but never seen one before.'

'A good many ranking Confederates carried them. Seems as if the inventor of the gun, a fellow named LeMat, was a Southern sympathizer.'

'Well, sonny, you'll need all the firepower you can pack if you're going to ride up and tell Fulton Armstrong you killed a couple of his bullies!' York grunted his cynicism. 'You best pay me in advance while you're here. Five dollars ought to cover the burial arrangements.' With a crooked grin. 'However, if you want to bequeath the gun to me, once you're dead, I'll consider that as payment for planting your sorry bones.'

Clancy ignored the offer, but did help him with the two bodies. Once done with that chore, he went to pick up his horse. It might not be a smart move, but he wanted to meet Fulton Armstrong. If he wasn't the man he was looking for, he had made a long trip for nothing. Well, he had managed to kill a couple of bullies and probably saved a young farmer's life. That had to count for something.

4

Jenny's mind hadn't developed to keep abreast with her years, but she was more impressionable and aware of other people's feelings than an ordinary six-year-old child.

'You mad at Jenny for sum'tin?' she asked, after Kate had driven the buggy for a mile without saying a word. Jenny often referred to herself in the third person. Kate felt it had something to do with her lack of confidence when it came to being understood. Shy, often to the point of shutting people out, her sister was outside the norm in a number of ways.

'No, Jenny,' Kate replied at once. 'I just have a lot on my mind.'

'Papa seems unhappy too.'

'It's a difficult time for us. We lost a lot of cattle when Choctaw was shot and killed, and Father's health isn't too good. You know how he sleeps a lot.'

'Will you buy me a sugar stick?' Her sister changed the subject abruptly. She often avoided sensitive topics. 'Jenny hasn't had any candy in a long time.'

'I think we can manage a . . . ' Kate paused in mid-sentence as she noticed Dolly, the single horse pulling their chaise, was suddenly limping. Having come down a long incline and with a sizable hill to climb in front of them, she stopped the mare, set the brake, and climbed down to check on her.

'What's the matter, Kate?' Jenny wanted to know. 'Why did you stop?'

But Kate hurried to the horse and lifted up the front foot she was favoring. There was nothing stuck under the iron shoe embedded in the hoof. She could see nothing wrong.

She led Dolly forward a couple steps, but the mare did an ungainly three-legged jump, unwilling to put any weight on the foot.

'It looks like Dolly has come up lame,' Kate told Jenny. 'We'll have to walk back to the ranch and get some help.'

'OK,' Jenny said quickly. 'I'll race you to the top of the hill.'

Before Kate could object, Jenny made a clumsy leap from the buggy and landed awkwardly on the side of her right foot. She cried out in pain and went right to the ground.

'Jenny!' Kate ran quickly to her. 'Are you all right?'

'Owie!' Jenny wailed. 'My foot hurts!'

Kate quickly examined her leg and, indeed, she had twisted her ankle. The area visible above her shoe was already turning red and would soon begin to swell.

'You can't walk all the way back to the ranch on an injured foot,' Kate said.

'Jenny is like Dolly, isn't she?' her sister lamented. Then, at Kate's curious look, 'Both of us got ouchies at the same time.'

'Yes, little sister, you both have a hurt leg.' Kate looked down and up the trail. They were in a hollow between two

63

hills, so she couldn't see very far in either direction. It hardly mattered, as only someone going to or coming from their ranch would be using the trail. She saw a couple of Armstrong's ranch hands go by, on their way into town earlier, but she didn't know when to expect them back. Besides, there was the possibility that they would use the secondary trail on their return trip. It was a more direct route to where Armstrong had built his bunkhouse and was completing the construction of his new home.

'We can't sit here all day long waiting for someone to come by, Jenny. I'm going to help you get in the buggy, then I'll walk home and get us another horse. I'll find Owens or Inger and bring them back to take care of Dolly, while we continue into town.'

'You gonna leave me here . . . alone?' Jenny asked in a timorous voice.

'It won't be for long. I can walk it in thirty or forty minutes. It shouldn't be more than an hour until I can get back.'

Jenny frowned. 'That sounds like a long time.'

Kate removed the timepiece she carried in her purse and held it out for Jenny to see. 'This small hand moves very slowly, but the bigger hand moves with every minute that passes. See where it is, right there on the number one? You watch. By the time it moves all the way around to the twelve I'll be back with help.'

Jenny didn't look convinced, but managed to get back into the buggy, with Kate doing a lot of lifting and guiding. Even as Kate was about to explain about the time again, Jenny let out a squeal of delight.

'I seen it move!' she exclaimed. 'Just like you said, Kate.'

'Yes, and by the time it moves all the way around to the number twelve, I'll be back. I promise.'

Jenny still had a frightened look, but she gave her head a nod. 'I'll sit right here and wait for you. Jenny will watch the hand move until it reaches the number twelve.'

Kate patted her on the knee. 'I'll hurry as fast as I can,' she promised. Then she started off at a fast walk, going up the steady slope, apprehensive about leaving Jenny alone. The alternative was to sit there until someone came along, and that might be hours.

★ ★ ★

Clancy topped the rise on his dusky buckskin and continued down the wagon trail. He had gone but a short way when he spotted a carriage sitting at the bottom of the hill. Drawing closer, he spied a young woman sitting alone on the seat cushion. Seeing him, she immediately ducked her head and avoided looking in his direction.

Clancy continued until his horse was level with the buggy. Then he stopped his gelding and gave the girl a closer look. She still had her head lowered, but he could make out her features. The honey-colored hair was quite short and trapped under a bonnet. Her dress appeared more befitting a child than a young woman. He observed that her facial features were also unusual, with round rosy cheeks, an almost non-existent chin and almond-shaped eyes. Her arms and legs appeared a bit shorter than those of an average person, too.

'Hi there,' he greeted her gently. 'Are you all right?'

The girl lifted her head ever so slightly but did not make eye contact. 'Jenny is waiting for Kate. Kate went to get help.'

Clancy realized that the girl was almost childlike, in spite of her size. He softened his voice, attempting to put her at ease. 'Did the buggy break down, Jenny?'

'Dolly has a sore leg.' She indicated the horse. Then, with a slight shrug of her shoulders, 'Jenny has a sore leg too.'

Clancy dismounted from Nugget and let the reins fall to the ground. When he stepped around to look at the girl, she peeked at him shyly. She was obviously nervous about being alone with a stranger, so he offered a friendly smile.

'I was on my way up to the Diamond T ranch. Is that where you're from?'

The girl's head nodded slightly. 'It's called the Big Diamond ranch,' she corrected him.

'You said you were hurt?'

Jenny lifted her right foot up enough for him to see an angry, bluish discoloration about her ankle.

'Bet that hurts,' he sympathized. 'Did you step wrong and twist your ankle?'

'Jenny jumped down from the buggy and hurt it.'

Clancy went through his saddle-bags until he found the strip of cloth, the kind soldiers carried for a field dressing. He showed it to Jenny.

'I can wrap your foot so it won't hurt as much. Would that be all right?'

She ducked her head again, but moved her foot slightly in his direction.

'I used to be in the army,' he explained, talking to help soothe her

68

fears. 'Lots of guys would twist a foot or turn their ankle while we were marching. We used this kind of bandaging technique to make it less painful to walk.'

Jenny remained silent, even as he removed her shoe and stocking. Then he applied the bandage to support her ankle by going around the leg, under her foot and above her heel. He finished by tearing the last of the strip enough to tie it above her injured ankle.

'Is that too tight?'

Jenny gave her head a negative shake, so he gingerly replaced her sock and shoe.

'Does that feel any better?'

The girl gently moved her foot from side to side and then pressed it against the floor of the carriage. A slight smile curled her lips.

'You must be a doctor,' she said.

'Not me. But I did share a room with a doctor for a couple weeks. He let me read a lot of his journals.' When she said nothing to that, he introduced himself.

'I'm Morgan Clancy. And you must be Jenny.'

'Uh-huh,' was her soft reply.

'And you said Kate went to get help,' he continued. 'Is Kate your mother?'

She made another of those timid smiles, as if he had said something funny. 'Kate is Jenny's sister. Kate takes care of Jenny.'

'I see,' Clancy said. 'So Kate went for help because the horse hurt its leg?'

'Uh-huh.'

'Is it a long way back to your house?'

'I dunno.'

'Do you know how long it will be before your sister returns?'

Jenny proudly held up a watch. 'Kate said she would be back when this watch hand is on the number twelve. Kate left me when it was on the number one.'

Clancy glanced at it and saw that Kate had been gone for less than ten minutes.

He walked round to the horse and could see she was favoring her front foot. After a short examination he began to unharness Dolly.

'Jenny, do you want to surprise your sister?' he asked, while continuing to work.

'How?'

'If you will allow me, I'll use my horse to pull the buggy. We can hurry back and pick up Kate so she doesn't have to walk all the way home. It looks like it's mostly uphill.'

'Yay! That would be fun.'

He turned the draft animal loose and stripped the saddle and tack from his own mount. After placing his gear in the rear boot of the chaise, he put Nugget into harness and then climbed aboard. Sitting down next to Jenny, he released the brake and turned the buggy around.

'Your horse must like you a lot.'

'Why is that?' Clancy asked her.

'Because he stood there the whole time you were moving Dolly. You didn't tie him up and yet he never once walked away.'

'Nugget is a good horse,' Clancy

71

agreed. 'He stands ground-reined as good as any horse I ever owned.'

Once he had Nugget moving at a quick pace, he looked over at Jenny.

'That's a real pretty dress you're wearing,' he said, making an effort to keep the girl from feeling uncomfortable about riding with a stranger.

'Kate made it.'

'Your sister sounds like a real nice girl.'

'Kate takes care of Jenny,' she repeated the phrase. 'We were gonna get some sugar sticks at the store.'

'I reckon you'll still have time to go into town.'

Jenny gazed at Clancy's horse. 'Nugget is a pretty horse. We don't have any of that color.'

'I call him Nugget, because of his color — kind of like a gold nugget — although he has black stockings and a little black on his ears.' He grinned at her. 'Kind of like he got covered in soot.'

She smiled a little.

'We should catch up with your sister in a few minutes.'

'I hope Kate isn't mad at Jenny. She said to wait for her.'

'Not to worry, Jenny. I'll tell her it was my idea. Besides, we'll save her a long walk. I'll bet we catch up with her long before the clock reaches the number twelve.'

A horsefly buzzed about Clancy's horse, then flew back and almost landed in Jenny's hair. Clancy waved a hand and swatted at it until it left.

'Jenny don't like flies!' the girl declared.

'Reminds me of my first job, when I was a little kid.' He cast a sidelong glance to see he had the girl's attention. 'I used to chase away flies from the horses that were tied outside the saloon. One day, some kid came up and started teasing me about my job. He said anyone could shoo flies.'

'Well, I told him that he couldn't shoo flies. And he got mad and said he could too. Then I said back, *no one can*

73

put shoes on a fly 'cause their feet are too small.'

He waited a moment and then Jenny began to giggle. 'That's silly,' she said.

'Not as silly as flies walking around wearing shoes.'

'You're funny,' Jenny said, looking at him with her dark eyes aglow.

Clancy didn't have to reply to that, as he spotted a woman walking brusquely on the trail ahead. 'Is that your sister?'

Jenny peered up the road. 'Uh-huh, that's Kate.'

The young woman heard the carriage approach and turned around to see who was on the trail. She frowned, seeing a strange man riding alongside her younger sister. However, she quickly masked the expression so that Jenny wouldn't see her disapproval.

'Howdy,' Clancy greeted her, as he pulled on the reins and stopped the carriage. 'You must be Miss Kate.'

'This man rescued Jenny,' her sister said quickly. 'He doctored my leg and said his horse could pull the buggy. Is that OK?'

Kate was a proper-looking girl, with shoulders erect and the slight build of a woman who kept busy physically. Her hair was a little darker than Jenny's blonde locks, with most of her flattering mane pulled tightly up under a woman's riding-hat. Dressed in calico, she had lace-up shoes and was obviously winded from walking up the steady incline. Her rich chestnut-brown eyes continued to glow with disapproval, but she displayed a smile for Jenny's sake.

'How very gallant of you, sir, to rescue my sister.'

'Name is Morgan Clancy,' he told her.

'Kate Freeman,' she replied curtly.

'I didn't know how far your place was, Miss Freeman,' he explained to excuse his brash actions. 'Your draft mare has a stone bruise, but I reckon she will make her way back to the barn by tonight. Be less of a strain on her by not pulling a carriage.'

'We were on our way into town. I don't know if we'll have time to round up another horse and still make the trip and back.'

Clancy tipped his hat with his free hand, holding the reins with the other. 'If you would permit me, I'd be happy to run you into town. I'm not in any hurry.'

'You promised I could have a sugar stick, Kate,' Jenny said. 'It's been a long time since Jenny had any candy.'

Kate climbed aboard, sitting on the opposite side of her sister. 'I shouldn't impose on you, Mr Clancy,' she said. 'I don't even know you.'

Clancy didn't argue, but pulled the reins and turned his horse around. Soon they were headed back to town.

'Been a long while since I was out for a buggy ride with a couple of beautiful girls,' he said, winking at Jenny. 'I'll be the envy of every man for miles around, escorting the two of you.'

Kate busied herself returning her

timepiece to her purse. Then she was forced to admire Clancy's handiwork as Jenny showed her the neatly wrapped ankle. She turned her foot from side to side and remarked: 'It don't hardly hurt at all, not since Mr Clancy bandaged it.'

'You've done some doctoring then?' Kate asked.

'I was in the war, Miss Freeman. Most of us learned a little about how to help those who had fallen or been hurt. There weren't a lot of doctors out on the battlefields or while marching from one place to another.'

'What brings you to Bluestone?'

'I heard there might be a job or two open at one of the ranches. I never had much to do with cattle, but I'm a quick learner.'

'You're talking about working at our ranch.'

He was more than a little surprised. 'Your ranch?'

'My father owns the Big Diamond ranch, although a new partnership is going to change the name to the Diamond T ranch.'

'Then your pa has taken on a partner. Is that it?'

Kate did not mask her concern. 'Something like that.'

'This partner, is he from around these parts?'

'No, Fulton Armstrong arrived about a year ago. We are unable to make the mortgage payment, because one of our riders was killed and a bunch of our steers was stolen. The sale of those cattle would have kept the ranch going. Now it appears as if only a partnership with Armstrong can save our ranch.'

'That strike you a bit odd,' Clancy kept the suspicion out of his voice, 'your cattle being rustled so soon after a second rancher takes up residence?'

'We've lost a few head to Indians and rustlers before, but never so many at one time. The theft has ruined us.'

The timeframe fitted. The rustled cattle were likely the beef that Rusty had delivered to the railhead for shipping. Clancy felt a rush of apprehension. Fulton Armstrong could be Sergeant Fuller's new identity.

'You said you were looking for a job?' Kate queried, when he failed to carry forward the conversation.

'Yes, but I'm not sure how happy Armstrong will be to see me. I had a run-in with a couple of his men in town.' He regarded the lady with an apologetic countenance. 'I believe I shortened his payroll by two cowhands.'

She frowned. 'You did what?'

'Well, you see, Miss Freeman, it was one of those baffling situations that just happens sometimes.'

'Explain how baffling,' she said, staring at him with an intense interest.

'There was this farmer fella in town — Darren Baker?'

'Yes, I know Darren.'

'Well, these two jokers — Gillum and Quint were the names given — they knocked Baker to the ground and were kicking the holy hel . . . uh,' he corrected quickly, when he realized

79

Jenny was also listening to his story, 'I mean, they were kicking the stuffings out of the poor kid. I stepped in to stop them and the fight took a more deadly twist.' He kept his eyes on the trail to avoid seeing the lady's disgust. 'I'm afraid those two jokers have bullied their last victim.'

'You killed them? Both of them?'

'It was either that or allow them to put holes in parts of my body I would as soon keep intact.'

Kate was silent for a few moments. Then she said: 'You must be very brave . . . or very stupid, Mr Clancy. Why else would you risk your life by going to see Mr Armstrong?'

'You figure he might take exception over my being forced to kill a couple of his hands?'

'*Exception!*' She laughed. 'You have a curious way of understating the seriousness of the situation.'

'It's like I told you, miss. I only come to Bluestone Creek to ask about a job.'

'One of Armstrong's best men has

gone to Denver to hire another couple men. He should be back any day. I'm sure they will take the place of Gillum and Quint. As far as I could tell, those two did little more than harass the farmers anyway.'

'That man who supposedly went to Denver? His name wouldn't be Jocko or something like that?'

The girl pinned him with an inquisitive gaze. 'Did he tell you to come here about a job?'

Clancy grimaced, wondering how smart it was to tell this girl all that had happened. He knew nothing about her, only that her father was entering into a joint enterprise with Armstrong. To her credit, it did seem that the partnership was being forced upon her family.

There isn't much use in lying, he thought. *It isn't as if I actually have a chance of being hired by Armstrong.*

'Jocko was in Kansas City when I was there a couple weeks back. He had brought in about a hundred head of steers and shipped them from the stockyards.'

The news brought a dark scowl to the woman's otherwise comely features. 'A hundred head of cattle?' she repeated angrily. 'Jocko was there to sell a hundred head of cattle!'

'That's right. I happened to be in the saloon when he was trying to recruit a cowhand to work for Armstrong.'

'The miserable, underhanded swine!' Kate cried. 'That's why no one on the ranch has seen Jocko for the last couple of months! Armstrong must have hired some rustlers to help him. Jocko killed Choctaw and stole our cattle!'

'Is something the matter, Kate?' Jenny asked, showing an immediate concern that her sister was so upset.

'It's nothing, Jenny.' Kate curbed her rage at once. 'I didn't mean to raise my voice.'

Clancy pointed to a black-and-white bird that was perched on a nearby bush. 'Jenny, do you know what kind of bird that is?'

Jenny looked at the bird and her face lit up. 'It's a magpie! There are lots of them around the ranch.'

'They ever wake you up in the morning with their loud chirping?' Clancy asked. 'The noise they make is like listening to a couple cats fighting.'

'Jenny's got a kitty,' the girl said, abruptly changing the subject. 'I call her Mittens, 'cause her two front paws are white.'

He softened his expression and said, 'I bet you're a good mommy.'

Jenny lowered her head shyly, but smiled. 'Uh-huh, Jenny is a good mommy. Mittens is a good kitty too.' She took a fleeting look his direction. 'Jenny has a dog too. His name is Shakes.'

'That's an odd name for a dog,' Clancy said, encouraging a reply.

'It's 'cause he always shakes when I hold him.'

Kate inserted an explanation. 'The dog's whole body shakes when he wags his tail.' Then she added, with a wry smile, 'And he does tend to shake when Jenny pulls him around in her little wagon.'

Clancy laughed. 'I understand completely, Jenny. Shakes sounds like a good name for the dog.'

As the younger girl seemed content again he glanced at Kate. She had a curious look on her face. It shone with a mixture of amazement and gratitude. However, when she spoke again, she was serious.

'If I were to contact the US marshal, would you testify in court against Jocko?'

'I probably wouldn't be the best witness for a court trial against him.'

'Why not?'

'Well, I did kill two of Armstrong's men in a gunfight not more than an hour ago.'

'You were saving Darren's life.'

'I'm a perfect stranger in town too. I don't know anyone west of the Kansas border.'

Kate regarded him with a stern look.

'Are you saying you won't speak up to help convict Jocko of stealing our cattle?'

'No, I'm saying there isn't any point.'

Her temper flared again. 'Give me one good reason why not!'

Clancy sighed. There was no way in the world to make what he had to say sound good. Kate stared at him, awaiting an answer. As there was little to do other than tell the truth he did just that.

'Jocko was killed by a shotgun blast to the chest.'

The news alarmed the young lady. 'Jocko is dead too?' She gasped in wonder. 'But when did that happen?'

'About two seconds after he shot at me!'

5

Stony and Bess were shocked to see their son's puffy face when Darren arrived with the supplies. Bess immediately took him into the house to treat his cuts and bruises, while Stony unloaded the goods and put away the team. By the time Stony had finished Darren was cleaned up and didn't look too bad, except his features appeared misshapen because of the swelling about his face that had closed one eye.

'I warned you to stay away from Armstrong's crew,' Stony told his boy.

'They were not in town by accident,' Darren replied. 'Gillum and Quint were there and waiting for me. I tried to avoid trouble, but they wouldn't let me get to the wagon.'

'You're lucky they let you leave town alive.'

Darren shook his head. 'It was not luck on my part, Pa. Some guy stepped in and stopped them from kicking me to death. I was on the ground and figured I'd seen my last sunset, when some fella took a hand.'

'Did you know him?'

'Never seen him before, but he could sure handle himself. He knocked both Gillum and Quint down, then tried to talk them out of a fight. When they grabbed for their guns, he shot them both dead.'

His mother gasped in shock. Stony was equally incredulous. He exclaimed, 'Gillum and Quint are dead?'

'The guy didn't waste any lead — one bullet each.'

Stony sat down on a kitchen chair. 'This is bad.'

'Not as bad as Darren being beaten to death!' Bess told her husband. 'They would have killed him! They would have killed our son for no reason whatsoever!'

'I need to speak to this man who saved your life.'

'The guy had me help him move the bodies out of the street. Then, as I was leaving town, he went over to see Mr York about tending to the two bodies.'

'You get his name?'

'Clancy is all I heard. I don't know if it's his first or last name.'

'I'll ride into town tomorrow and talk to him. If Armstrong thinks we sent for a gunman to join our side, he might retaliate.'

'I'm sure Hank will tell him the guy just happened to be in town. I mean, he was in the store while I was loading the supplies. He was just a customer when the trouble started.'

Stony bobbed his shaggy head. 'I'll still ride into town and speak to him. If for no other reason, I'll thank him for saving your life.' With another look of dread he added, 'And I'll warn him to get out of the country.'

★ ★ ★

Ringer entered the house and found Armstrong at his desk. 'Arno just rode in, boss. He says Gillum and Quint are both dead.' Armstrong's mouth fell open and Ringer continued, 'They were knocking the Baker kid around and some wandering saddle tramp butted in. It came to gunplay and the stranger downed them both.'

'I don't believe it,' Armstrong replied. 'Gillum was no slouch with a gun. And Quint knew which end to point, too.'

Ringer handed him a piece of paper. 'This isn't going to make you any happier either. It's a telegraph message from the mortuary in Kansas City. They are notifying you that Jocko was buried last week. He had enough money on him to cover their services.'

Armstrong was dumbfounded. 'How can that be? Jocko sent a wire saying he had finished the job and was about to head back.'

'Lucky he deposited the money,' Ringer said. 'We've got bills to pay.'

Armstrong swore. 'Gillum and Quint

killed in town. Now Jocko is six feet underground! I expected him back with two or three men any day. I can't believe he went and got himself killed!'

'It probably took a while for the mortician to figure out who Jocko was working for. Only the buyer at the stockyard knew where you could be reached. They must have tracked him down, but it took a few days.'

'Did you learn anything else? How did Jocko end up in a shoot-out?'

'Some bartender called him by his old name. He tried to kill the barkeep, but the man behind the counter fired back with a shotgun. That's all the telegraph message said, other than that no charges were brought against the bartender. Rusty had shot at him first.'

'This is going to leave us mighty short-handed, Ringer. We've only got four men left drawing fighting wages and three regular cowhands to manage our herd. It leaves us in a bind until we take over Freeman's ranch.'

'He's still got two riders working for

him. That will give us five men to handle the cattle. We can manage.'

'Oh, yeah.' Armstrong uttered a cynical grunt. 'Except one of Freeman's men might spot one of the beeves with an altered brand that didn't make the trip to Kansas!'

'Arno did a pretty good job with the running iron, boss. It's hard to tell that the brand's been altered.'

'A good cowhand would spot it in a minute. Both Owens and Ingersoll are old hands at branding.'

'So how can we drive out the farmers and tend our cattle too?'

'We'll have to let the farmers be.' Armstrong did some quick thinking. 'I'll persuade Tom to move up the wedding date. Once I have the contract signed, we'll have control of his ranch and all of the land and cattle that go with it. We'll fire his two riders and hire some new men for next year's round-up.'

'What do you want to do about the drifter?'

'Kill him.'

* * *

Kate collected a few items and gave the storekeeper a list of needed supplies for the ranch. While Hank began gathering the stuff to fill her order, his wife, Maggie, patiently helped Jenny with her choice of candy. The girl was having a hard time making up her mind.

Clancy was looking over the ammunition available when Kate slipped across to him.

She kept her voice down so that Jenny would not overhear her speaking. 'You didn't say why Jocko tried to kill you.'

'He was a guard at Andersonville,' Clancy informed her. 'Have you heard the stories about that prison camp?'

'No. The town has a newsletter that is published each week, but it is only one page and doesn't cover much of anything that's going on across the country. Once my two older brothers were killed, fighting for the Union, we

92

no longer wanted to hear about the war.'

Clancy expressed his regret for her loss and quickly gave her some background on the abominable treatment of the soldiers. He told her how his brother had been one of the many victims.

'When I called Jocko by the name he used as a Confederate soldier, he tried to kill me. I was working as a bartender and the only gun available was a scatter-gun the owner kept under the bar. I had hoped to question Rusty and learn where I could find Sergeant Fuller.'

Kate's eyebrows drew closer together and she concluded, 'You think Armstrong is Sergeant Fuller!'

'It's a possibility. I was told he arrived last year, shortly after Andersonville was closed down, and he had money to spend. He could be the man I'm looking for.'

'I'm supposed to marry Armstrong and merge our ranch with his,' Kate informed him. 'My father is bound by his word, considering the man has agreed to help us pay the mortgage this year.'

'If the man is Sergeant Fuller, the money he came here with was blood money, gold from dead men's teeth and every coin, dollar or valuable he could steal from their lifeless bodies. Add to that, the money he's offering to help with your mortgage payment is from the sale of your own rustled cattle.' Clancy could not keep the vehemence from his words. 'If Armstrong is the man I'm looking for, you won't have to worry about any wedding.'

'Unless he kills you,' she reminded him. 'You've already put three of his men in the grave. I'm sure he's going to be more than a little interested in who you are and why you came to Bluestone.'

Jenny interrupted, having come over to join them. 'Kate,' the girl pleaded softly. 'Can I have three pieces of candy? Jenny can't choose just one.'

Kate rallied a stern expression, but there was little doubt she always gave Jenny what she wanted. 'On one condition.' Jenny gave a quick nod. 'You can only eat one piece today. You must save the others for another day.'

'I promise,' Jenny said, matching Kate's somber expression. 'Jenny will only eat one and keep the other two for later.'

Kate gave her the go-ahead and Jenny, still favoring her ankle, hurried back to the counter.

'I read something about a condition some children are born with,' Clancy told Kate. 'It was in a medical journal.'

'Jenny's condition?'

'An English physician, by the name of John Down, studied a number of children who suffered a form of slow and unusual development. He termed the condition as a syndrome and wrote that the special children were usually born to older mothers who were pretty much near the end of their child-bearing years. He determined that these children shared the same facial features and body types, while being limited in their mental learning capacity. He also described them as being mongoloid in appearance, though I'm not sure what he meant by that.'

'Mongoloid?'

Clancy didn't remark on the description. 'Anyway, the medical society considers his findings to be worthwhile enough that they have named the condition after the man's last name. Children born within his guidelines are to be deemed as suffering from the Down Syndrome.'

'I was with Father in Denver once and we saw a young boy who had similar features to Jenny's,' Kate said. 'But I didn't know there were enough of them so as to be lumped into a group or category.'

'This Doctor John Down evidently studied a substantial number of cases. He stated that the mental limits of each child seemed to be influenced by how the family accepted and treated them.

Some who were put into asylums or were shunned by their families tended to be severely limited in their learning. Those who received love and support often grew to a point equal to that of a normal 10 to 13-year-old. A few were even able to work outside the home.'

Kate gazed at Clancy with a mysterious expression. 'You are the strangest man I ever met.'

Clancy grinned. 'That's good . . . right?'

The girl ignored his comment. 'You calmly tell me you are responsible for the deaths of three of Armstrong's men, while you communicate with Jenny with the gentleness of a man who has been around children all his life. Now you spout research about some physician who has put a name to Jenny's lack of maturity.'

'Well, I didn't start out to kill any of those men; Jenny is about as sweet as a honeycomb; and I just happened to read some medical journals while I was rooming with an army surgeon.'

'Yes, but I . . . just . . . ' She didn't continue. Instead, she quickly turned and walked to the counter, where Jenny was making her final selection of candy sticks.

Clancy wondered if it had been a mistake to mention Jenny's condition. Kate was obviously protective of her and he was an outsider. He had thought that sharing what he had learned might be a comfort to the woman. She would know that her sister was not unique, that her malady was the same as that of a number of other children.

Good luck telling a gal what you think she needs to hear, Clancy, he chided himself. *Trying to figure out a woman is like trying to make a chocolate cake out of road apples.*

★ ★ ★

Ringer was puzzled when he saw the horse limping along the road leading up to the Big Diamond ranch. He recognized it as the one Kate usually used for her trips to town. He expected to find the wagon on the road and perhaps Kate too. However, he saw nothing as he continued down to where the ranch trail met up with the main rode into town.

Turning around, he rode back up the familiar pathway until he spied a good place to set up an ambush. Angling along the side of the hill, he eased his horse through the trees until he came to a little brush-covered knoll. He dismounted and tethered his mount in a cove and out of sight. With rifle in hand, he made his way to a spot that allowed him to see the road clearly. At a distance of fifty yards he would have no trouble putting a bullet in the man who had gunned down Gillum and Quint.

The idea that the drifter would make the ride up to see the boss was ridiculous. But Arno had said that was the man's intention. Arno had talked to Hank at the store and the fellow had asked directions to their ranch. What kind of man killed a man's hired help and then rode up to visit with him?

As he sat idly his mind shifted to Jocko. The report said a bartender had called him by name . . . meaning Rusty. Perhaps it was someone who knew him from before the war. He immediately dismissed that notion. There was only one reason Jocko would have tried to kill the bartender. The man serving bar had to be someone who recognized Jocko from the war and almost certainly knew he had been a prison guard at Andersonville. Whoever called him by name wasn't an ex-Confederate soldier. It would have been someone who wanted revenge. The scenario that made the most sense was: the barkeep must have been a Yankee prisoner who had been interned at the prison compound.

A single horse-drawn buggy appeared on the trail. Ringer saw it was Freeman's chaise with his two daughters on board. However, they weren't alone. The rig was pulled by a buckskin horse with black stockings, one he'd never seen before. The man driving was a capable-looking gent, with a flat-crowned, wide-brimmed hat covering most of his face. Ringer knew that both of Freeman's ranch hands were off working with cattle, so who the devil was this guy? And why was he driving Kate and Jenny home?

Ringer made the decision to ride into town. The gent who had killed Quint and Gillum must have changed his mind. He didn't intend to sit and wait in ambush for a rider who might never appear. He would slip into town and question Hank about this new arrival. Then he would inform Armstrong and they could decide the best way to deal with him.

6

Thomas Freeman hobbled out on the porch at the sound of their approaching carriage. Scraggy and frail-looking, he used a cane for support, but his eyes were alive and measured. No beard covered his chin, but his sideburns grew well below his ears.

Clancy stopped a few feet from the front of the house and jumped down. He offered a helping hand to Jenny as she got down from the chaise. Placing his hands at her hips, he lifted her down gently. He would have done the same for Kate, but she hurriedly descended from the other side of the carriage and moved forward to face her father.

'I was worried about you two,' the elderly gent said sternly. 'Dolly come into the yard a few minutes ago, hopping along like a three-legged dog. I didn't know what to think.'

Kate explained about the stone bruise and how Clancy had arrived to take them to town and back. Jenny also had to show her father Clancy's handiwork, proudly displaying her wrapped ankle. Tom suggested she spend the day resting her foot so the swelling would go down.

Clancy kept busy while the family conversed. He unharnessed Nugget and then replaced the saddle and tack, making the cinch secure for riding again. He didn't offer a word until he finished with the chore.

'Where would you like the buggy, Mr Freeman?' he asked.

'Round to the side of the house in the lean-to, so it will be protected from the weather.'

Clancy pulled the chaise around and backed it under the shelter. He returned to find that Kate was the only one still outside the house. She regarded him with a sphinxlike intensity. It caused him to wonder what kind of impression he had made on her.

Judging by the mysterious appraisal, she was likely undecided.

'Father says to ask you to stay for supper. It's getting late, so you're welcome to spend the night in the bunkhouse.'

'Give my thanks to your pa for the invite, but I need to get back to town. I've got to send a telegraph message and wait for the reply. It might take some time.'

The girl stepped closer and visibly took a deep breath. 'I owe you a debt of thanks for coming to our rescue today,' she said. 'You were very gallant.'

Clancy chuckled. 'Never been called that before.'

'You tended to my little sister's injury and spent your whole day escorting us back and forth. You didn't have to do that.'

'Meeting Jenny was a pleasure, Miss Freeman,' he told her truthfully. 'And it was a privilege, not a chore, being your escort. You provided me with the best company I've had since before the war.'

Kate's complexion darkened a shade and she shifted her feet nervously. 'Well,' she murmured, 'I just wanted to thank you for your courtesy.'

'I'll be seeing you again,' he promised. 'First off, I need to get some more information on Armstrong. Whether he is Sergeant Fuller or not, it's pretty much a certainty he is behind the rustling of your cattle and killing your hired hand.'

'I don't know what good that will do,' she replied. 'We don't have any law hereabouts and I don't know if the US marshal will want to make a trip all the way to Bluestone to investigate.'

'I'll save him the trouble, if Armstrong is the man I'm looking for.'

'You can't be thinking of going up against him alone?'

Clancy didn't have an answer for that yet. 'I'd better wait and see what I can find out, before I open my big mouth too wide and end up eating my words.'

'You're risking your life being here. After killing two of Armstrong's men, he might send someone to kill you.'

'This Armstrong jackal, does he happen to have any scars on his face?'

Kate frowned. 'He has a little one above his eye . . . kind of a half-circle.'

With no little effort, Clancy hid the immediate rush of excitement her answer caused.

It's him! Sergeant Fuller!

As Nugget had been standing patiently, Clancy took hold of the reins and moved around to mount up. He paused to smile at the lady one more time. 'Like I said, it's been a real pleasure meeting you and Jenny.'

'Perhaps I will see you again,' Kate responded. It could have been wishful thinking on his part, but her words sounded more like an invitation than a parting remark.

Clancy touched the rim of his hat in a polite gesture of farewell and stepped aboard Nugget. Nudging his horse lightly with his heels, he rode out of the yard and back down the lane toward town.

★ ★ ★

Kate's father was waiting for her inside
the house. He had taken his usual place
in the easy chair and looked past her
when she came into the room.

'Your friend didn't stay for supper?'

'No, Father. He had something to do
in town.'

'Jenny was all smiles,' Tom remarked,
his affection for his younger daughter
evident in the warmth of his voice. 'She
showed off her bandaged ankle as if it
was a birthday gift.'

'Yes, Mr Clancy was incredibly good
with her.'

'Seems a gentle and temperate man,'
Thomas praised.

'There is more than one side to Mr
Clancy,' Kate said. Then she told him
about the two rowdies from Armstrong's ranch beating up on Darren.
When she related that Clancy had
killed them both, his jaw almost became
unhinged. Next, she repeated what he
had told her about Jocko, along with

the fact that Armstrong was very probably behind the rustling of their cattle. Thomas barely controlled his rage as she finished.

'That means that that no-good, worthless, redheaded coyote killed Choctaw!' He swore under his breath. 'No wonder Armstrong asked to move up the wedding.'

'He what?'

'Yes.' Thomas was shamefaced. 'And I said I would speak to you about it tonight.'

'If Jocko stole those cattle, he did it on Armstrong's orders.'

'Don't you think I know that, daughter? I've been so worried about dying and leaving you girls alone, I was ready to do anything . . . even let myself be talked into a partnership with a murdering scoundrel!'

'We have no proof,' Kate reminded him. 'You can't say anything to warn Armstrong. If he knew Clancy was looking into the stolen cattle and suspected that he was the sergeant from

Andersonville, he would send his men to kill him.'

'Andersonville?'

Kate related the details as to why Clancy had come to Colorado and how he had killed Jocko over in Kansas City.

'The man has been busy,' her father said, not hiding his incredulity.

'Yes, but we must not let on that we know why he is here in Bluestone.'

'That might be difficult, Kate, being as you let him drive you and Jenny into town and back.'

'He was being a Good Samaritan,' she countered. 'With Jenny along, most people would think there was little chance we would talk about anything as serious as murder and rustling.'

'All right,' Thomas concurred. 'We'll keep quiet and pretend to go along with this whole marriage thing . . . for now.'

'It's the safest way to proceed.'

'I only hope your newfound friend doesn't get himself killed. Now that we know the truth about Choctaw and our beef, there's no way I'm going to let you marry that murdering thief!'

★   ★   ★

It was dark before Ringer reached the nearly finished ranch house. Armstrong had hired several carpenters to work on the place. The sitting room, kitchen and one bedroom were intact and the entire roof and walls were in place. All that was needed was to finish up the second bedroom and back porch. He had put the last bit of work on hold, having run out of money and awaiting the funds from their sale of the stolen beef in Kansas City.

Ringer put away his horse and found Armstrong sitting in his favorite leather-bound easy chair. He had a cigar burning, lying in a plate he kept beside him on a small bookcase. There was also his usual bottle of bourbon whiskey and a single shot-glass.

'Been wondering when you would get here,' Armstrong said. 'The cook left you some stew warming on the stove.'

'Good. I paid York for the burial of our two men, but left town without eating.'

'What'd you find out about the drifter?'

'We have a job for Flint and Cole.' Armstrong's expression clouded and Ringer continued; 'The name of the gent who put Gillum and Quint in a wooden box is none other than Morgan Clancy. You recognize the name, don't you?'

'Clancy,' Armstrong repeated. 'He must have discovered the mass grave at Andersonville.'

'No doubt about it, Boss. He's come looking for revenge.'

'If he's here in Bluestone he must be not satisfied that Wirz is going to be tried for the deaths of the men at the prison camp.'

'Got to wonder how he found us.'

'He must have learned about the ranch when he killed Rusty,' Armstrong deduced. 'But how did he know to take on Gillum and Quint?'

'Hank said Clancy was in the store buying supplies when our boys started pounding Darren Baker into the dust. He intervened and it came to gun play.'

'You said you wanted Flint and Cole to handle this, Ringer. Do you think they are the men for the job?'

'Yes. I would wager Morgan Clancy has come here to kill every man Jack who was at Andersonville. He's a man on a mission and the only thing that will stop him is a bullet through the heart.'

'How will the boys recognize him?'

'I saw him in the carriage with Kate and Jenny, but I didn't know who he was at the time. It looked as if he'd used his own horse to pull the buggy. It's a dark buckskin with black stockings — be real easy to spot — and he'll probably be coming up to see us tomorrow.'

'Soon as you have some chow, you head over to the bunkhouse and give the order to the boys. Wart and Arno are at the line shack tonight. They took supplies up to our three regular cowhands. Cole and Flint ate with me, so you can fill them in about setting up an ambush.'

'Good thing Kate's draft horse came up lame. Otherwise, Clancy would have showed up today.'

'Tell the boys to be down at the trail at first light. When Clancy comes riding this way a second time, they can put an end to his vendetta.'

'What about a story to cover the killing?' Ringer asked.

'I'll warn old man Freeman that we spotted a couple of renegade Indians out by our remuda, looking to steal a couple horses. We can say they bushwhacked Clancy for his horse.'

'I'll tell the boys to leave Indian sign on the body and get rid of the horse. That ought to do the trick.'

Armstrong rubbed the stubble along his chin. He had shaved off his beard so as not to be recognized and his face still felt naked. 'Do you think Clancy might have told someone else he suspects us?'

'I don't know, boss. Hank, being the snoop he is, went over to visit with York as soon as Clancy left his store with the Freeman girls. He said Clancy reported the deaths of Gillum and Quint to the marshal's office in Denver.'

'Smart action on his part. It doesn't give anyone a chance to turn him in for the shooting that way.'

'He will be a rock in our shoes until he's taken care of,' Ringer avowed.

Armstrong returned to their plan. 'There's still enough Indian trouble around, so that no one is going to question an attack. We'll have the boys cart the body into town and get rid of his horse. A couple of make-believe Cheyenne warriors will put an end to our worries about Morgan Clancy.'

Ringer uttered a sigh. 'By showing up here, the guy's left us no choice.'

'Our goal is in sight.' Armstrong tried to elevated his spirits. 'Once I get Kate in front of a parson and we sign that contract, we'll own this whole valley. I doubt Freeman will last long after that. As soon as he takes his last breath that big house will be yours. We'll add to our herd and rule this part of the country together.'

Ringer gave a nod of approval, but he was still concerned about Clancy. He knew they wouldn't be safe, not until that man was buried in his grave.

★　★　★

Flint and Cole set up on either side of the trail. Cole had a Henry rifle, while Flint was ready with a brand-new Winchester. Both of them were pretty good shots, and at a distance of less than thirty yards, they would be accurate and deadly.

It was close to noon when the two men spotted a lone rider coming up the trail. He rode a buckskin with black stockings and was dressed like a cowhand. His hat was tipped low to shade his face and the horse moved at a steady but unhurried gait. The two men

waited until he reached a level spot
— the one they had agreed upon — and
both of them fired at nearly the same
instant.

The horse danced about from the
sudden gunshots, while the man buck-
led in the middle and spilled out of the
saddle. He landed hard and flat, felled
by two bullets to his chest. Cole jumped
up and hurried forward, but the horse
whirled about and took off down the
trail.

'Stop him!' Cole shouted to Flint.

'I'm on foot too, you dummy!' Flint
snarled at him. 'What the hell are you
doing, running out of the brush
thataway?'

'I wanted to grab the animal before
he could head for the barn.'

Flint snickered. 'Tell me, smart guy,
how did that work out?'

'Yeah, yeah,' Cole growled back.
'Well, I didn't see you trying to catch
the blasted horse!'

'You remembered to bring that
Cheyenne arrow we found a few weeks

back, didn't you?'

'Right here, tucked in my belt,' Cole replied. 'I'll just shove it in one of the bullet holes and we'll take the body to town.'

'You fix the body,' Flint replied. 'I'll go round up another horse. I don't know about you, but I'm not going to ride double with a corpse.'

'Get a move on,' Cole said. 'Soon as I stick the arrow in this jasper I'll wait back off of the trail, out of sight, until you get back. There's a chance someone might have heard the shots.'

'If a rider comes along, you slip away and meet me on the upper trail. No need of us taking the body into town, not if someone else is around to do it.'

Cole agreed and went over to the body. The man was stone dead, so he found a bullet hole and pushed the arrow in until it hit bone. Then he broke a nearby branch from a large sagebrush and dusted away his foot-prints. When he was satisfied with how the scene looked, he returned to a secluded spot to wait for Flint to return.

* * *

Clancy was helping York fit a support bracket on a freight wagon, while awaiting an answer to a telegraph message, when Nugget arrived at the livery. Having been housed and fed in a forward stall the last two nights, it was where the horse chose to return.

It took only a glance to see there was blood on the saddle.

'This don't look good,' York spoke the obvious. 'That Texas boy sure 'nuff got himself ambushed!'

Clancy took the reins of his horse and affectionately rubbed her under the chin. 'It's my fault,' he said sadly. 'I lent him my mount and some bushwhacker thought it was me.'

'I didn't figure Armstrong would react so quick,' York said.

'We've got to go find Johnson. He could be hurt bad and need help.'

York put a hand on Clancy's arm to restrain him. 'I'll do the looking, sonny. You stay out of sight. If those coyotes discover they've killed the wrong man, they'll come looking for you.' He squinted up at Clancy. 'And if they don't know Johnson wasn't you, it's gonna be a whole lot safer for you to not be waltzing around where people can see you.'

The man had a point. Clancy gave a bob of his head and led Nugget into the barn. York saddled one of his three riding-horses and headed for the trail up to the Big Diamond ranch.

Clancy gave Nugget water, a small ration of oats and a little hay. Then he began using some of York's all-purpose solvent to try and clean the blood off the saddle. He wasn't having much luck when he heard steps at the barn entrance.

'Frosty?' a man's voice called out. 'Is that you back there?'

Clancy didn't recognize the man, but he was dressed as a farmer. Having been spotted, he couldn't very well duck down and hide.

'York had to run an errand,' he replied.

The farmer was middle-aged, with a floppy hat covering the upper portion of his face. The worn bib overalls were clean, but they had been patched about as many times as the average home-made quilt.

'Name's Stony Baker,' he introduced himself. 'I'm looking for a fellow named Clancy. Would that be you?'

Clancy set down the rag and solvent and walked over to meet the man. 'That's me, Morgan Clancy.'

Stony stuck out his hand and shook Clancy's arm like a vapor-locked water pump. 'I have to tell you, me and the wife can't thank you enough for saving our boy yesterday. Darren said those two men seemed intent upon killing him.'

'Why the hostility toward you?'

'We moved here from Missouri a couple years back. We had hoped to leave the war behind us. The Jenkins family lost a son and brother and the Callen family lost their oldest boy to the fighting. My own son is the last child at home for us and it was tough to keep him from joining in the fight. He's barely nineteen now, but we all wanted to save what little family we had left.'

'And Armstrong is trying to push you off your farms?'

Stony shook his head. 'He and several of his men arrived in Bluestone like they owned the world. They took root a mile or so from the Big Diamond ranch and began building a cattle ranch. We use a little of the water along the creek to irrigate when there's a dry spell. Armstrong says he'll be needing all of the water for his cattle and wants to run us off our land.'

'I rode along the creek for a mile or so,' Clancy replied. 'It's mid-autumn and there's still plenty of water. I don't see it running dry because of a little irrigation.'

'Darren said Quint and Gillum called

121

him a Reb, but I saw those boys when they rode in. Two or three of them were still carrying Confederate gear.'

'What part of Missouri are you farmers from?'

'Kansas City.'

'Makes perfect sense,' Clancy said. 'I believe Armstrong's real last name is Fuller. If I'm right, he came from the same part of the country as you folks. He could be afraid someone from your group will recognize him.'

'Why change his name? A good many soldiers deserted from both sides during the war. Far as I know, there's no one looking for any of them.'

Clancy told him a little about Andersonville and why he thought Fuller would change his name. He finished with, 'And now someone has killed an innocent man, thinking it was me.'

'Because you stood up for my boy.'

'Could be,' Clancy said. 'But Armstrong also might have an idea of why I'm here. York rode up to find Johnson's body — he's the cowhand I let borrow my horse this morning. He arrived without a cent to his name, so I thought I was doing him a favor.'

'Well, you surely did us a favor, saving our boy,' Stony said. 'If there's anything we can do to help, all you have to do is ask. We're not much good in a gunfight, but we will stand at your side.'

'I hope this doesn't come to a war. I'm only looking for one man.'

'Sometimes the rock you're searching for is at the bottom of the pile,' Stony spouted philosophically. 'The offer stands, if you find you need help uncovering the one stone you are after.'

7

Kate was crestfallen at the news. She sat down next to her father and struggled to hold back her tears.

'You're sure about this?' Thomas asked Ringer.

'We've seen a couple Indians in the area the last few days, but thought they had moved on. It appears those renegades ambushed the fellow on his way up here. Flint and Cole heard a shot and rode around the bend in time to see the guy fall from his horse. The Indians spooked when they saw them and the man's horse ran off toward town. It was a buckskin with black stockings.'

'Two Indians kill a man for his horse . . . then let the horse get away?' Thomas did not hide his disbelief at the story.

Ringer hurried on rather than

respond to his doubt. 'Flint gave chase, while Cole stopped to see if he could help the man. It was too late for them to help the drifter and the Indians managed to escape in the trees.'

'What did your men do with the body?' Kate wanted to know.

'Took him to town so York could tend to the burying. He might have an idea about who to contact about his death too.'

Jenny had been listening but she didn't speak. Instead, she came over and sat next to Kate. Oddly, she took hold of Kate's arm and squeezed gently.

'What happened between the Clancy fellow and Gillum and Quint?' Thomas changed the subject. 'We heard Clancy killed them both.'

'They got into some kind of scrap in town.'

'Are you sure your men weren't getting even with Clancy?' Kate asked the question point blank.

'If one of the boys killed Clancy, it wasn't on Armstrong's orders. As far as

125

Quint and Gillum goes, they were acting on their own when they got into the fight with Darren.'

'Two full-grown men gang up on a boy of nineteen,' Kate did not hide her disgust. 'That's certainly something to be proud of.'

Ringer glared at her impudence, but his voice remained under control. 'With our two men dead, we only have Baker's word as to what started the fight. The one thing we do know is that Clancy shot and killed them both.'

She did not back down. 'Hank said your men drew on Clancy when he stopped them from beating Darren Baker. He was defending himself.'

'It doesn't matter now one way or the other.' Ringer brushed off her comments. 'We've got a couple men searching the hills for those renegades. If they are still around, we'll find them.'

'Thanks for bringing us the news.' Thomas ended their visit.

Ringer didn't offer a farewell. He left

the room and went out to his waiting horse.

'It's too bad about your friend,' Kate's father said to her. 'He seemed like a good man, and he was about our last hope to save this ranch.'

'It wasn't Mr Clancy,' Jenny spoke up softly.

Kate regarded Jenny with a puzzled frown. 'What do you mean, Jenny?'

Thomas was also curious. He asked her, 'What makes you think the man shot wasn't Mr Clancy?'

The girl seemed embarrassed to have both of them waiting for her to speak. It took a few moments and a little gentle coaxing before she answered the question.

'Nugget ran away,' Jenny eventually explained her logic. 'Mr Clancy said Nugget was a good horse. When he took the harness off Dolly, Nugget stood and waited for him. He didn't have to tie him up or anything. Nugget was a good horse,' she repeated. 'He wouldn't have run away.'

'Maybe the men who attacked Clancy frightened him,' Thomas suggested. 'Any horse can be frightened.'

But Jenny remained adamant. 'Shakes wouldn't leave Jenny if I was hurt. Mittens wouldn't leave Jenny either.' She lifted her eyes enough to look at Kate. 'Nugget wouldn't leave Mr Clancy if he was hurt either.'

Kate rose to her feet, wanting to believe Jenny's logic. 'I'm going to town, Father. If Mr Clancy was killed, I need to know how he died. If Jenny is right, I'll find and have a word with Mr Clancy.'

'I reckon I should tell you to stay home and be safe,' her father said. 'But I know you're going to do what you're going to do . . . whether I like it or not.'

'I'm acting foreman on this ranch,' Kate affirmed with some pluck. 'If you doubt my claim, ask Owens or Ingersoll.'

'Have a safe trip, daughter.' Tom capitulated without further argument.

'Jenny and I will be here waiting for you.'

* * *

York snorted his contempt. 'Look at that.' He pointed at the arrow in Johnson's chest. 'A Cheyenne hunting arrow. We're supposed to think this was Injuns.'

Clancy eased the body over enough to look at his back. 'Two exit wounds . . . probably from a rifle.' Then, inspecting the man's chest, 'Make that two rifles. The angles of these wounds are from different sides.'

'Mighty good shooting for a couple renegade Injuns.'

'I'd say the two renegades responsible were wearing chaps and work for Armstrong.'

'Who do we notify about Mr Johnson's death?' York wanted to know.

'I only knew he had come up with a trail drive from Texas. He wasn't of a mind to go back as things are still pretty bad down there. I thought I was doing him a favor by sending him up to speak to Mr Freeman.'

Granny stepped out of the office and announced that a message was coming in for Clancy.

Both of them went into the office and waited, while Granny scribbled on a pad and then tapped out an answer. Clancy remained patient until the woman gave an ending sequence and signed off.

'The marshal says you're getting a lot of people killed with no positive results,' Granny said, summarizing the wire.

'I thought he might be a little irritated with me.'

'He also said that the cattle inspector noticed the T part of the brand had been added after the diamond shape was already on the cattle that Jocko sold. However, Jocko had told him the two ranches were being joined by a marriage and the new name would be the Diamond T ranch. That's how come he let it pass.'

'The brand inspector should have been a little curious as to why Jocko drove his cattle an extra hundred and fifty miles. Most cattle are being sold at Abilene, yet he continued to Kansas City.'

'Probably got a little more money per pound by shipping them from there,' York suggested. 'Jocko also might have figured the inspector wouldn't look as closely at beef being sold at a major shipping point.'

'He say anything about Johnson?'

Granny shook her head. 'Only that you ought to look into the murder and get back to him.'

'Sure feel bad about him,' Clancy said. 'He came all the way here just to get killed.'

'You say you met him in Missouri?' York queried.

'Yes. He arrived in Kansas with a bunch of other drovers at Abilene, then wandered as far as Kansas City looking for work. He lost most of his money at the saloons and chasing women . . . like a good many cowhands.'

York heaved a sigh of regret. 'Chuck, the stage driver, said he let Johnson ride shotgun for him, because the guy didn't have enough money for his fare.'

'Well, I'm not exactly flush with money, but I'll fork over the price of his burial.'

'How about you pay me for the wood and we dig the hole together?' York made a counter-proposal.

'Show me where you want the grave and I'll get started.'

★ ★ ★

Kate approached town and saw a couple men digging in the city cemetery. The graveyard was situated where it was out of sight from the main street. Located on a gentle slope, the entire burial site was surrounded by a short picket fence. As she drew closer, her heart leapt in her chest. The taller man looked like . . .

Kate's steed jumped in surprise at

the dig of her heels then responded, to gallop across the open ground. Kate yanked the animal's reins hard and had off-mounted before her horse had come to a complete stop. The two men ceased their work as she bolted through the gate and stopped a few feet away.

'What on earth are you doing alive!' she cried. 'And why are you working out in the open where you can be seen?'

Clancy paused to lean on his shovel and looked at York. 'Is she talking to you or to me?'

'Bah!' the smaller man growled. 'Ain't no female gonna worry about my worn-out carcass. It's your sorry bones the lady is worried about.'

Kate sputtered something about some men not having the brains of a wilted daffodil before she noticed a blanket-wrapped body.

'Who is the man you're burying?' she wanted to know. 'And why was he riding your horse?'

'Jumpin' horny toads!' York complained. 'You sound like one of them nagging wives I try to avoid. Who put the ants in your drawers?'

Kate glared at him, her teeth anchored and eyes flashing fire. York immediately grew silent, cowed by her rancor, and began to use the spade again.

'Hello again, Miss Freeman,' Clancy greeted the girl. 'May I say you're very attractive with your hair flowing free and a dash of color in your cheeks from a hard ride.'

'Ringer told us that you were dead.'

'I don't know anyone named Ringer.'

'He's Armstrong's foreman,' she explained. 'He said that you were killed by Indians this morning.'

Clancy was immediately serious. 'The man killed was named Johnson. I let him borrow my horse so he could speak to your father about a job. He was a cowhand from Texas and I knew you'd lost a man some weeks back.'

Kate calmed her whirlwind of emotions and self-consciously used both hands to smooth her hair and adjust her riding-hat. With renewed aplomb, she settled all of the fuss with a single 'Oh.'

'We took the back way out of town to prepare the grave,' Clancy advised her. 'I'm not so gullible as to think two renegade Indians attacked and killed Johnson for my horse.'

Kate's stern expression melted away, replaced by one of wonder. 'Jenny refused to believe it was you who had been shot, because your horse ran away. She's the reason I had to come and find out for myself.'

'I could take your concern to mean you have developed a liking for me.'

The softness and worry disappeared from her face. 'It's only natural to not wish any harm come to someone who went out of their way to help during a time of need. You rescued Jenny and me when our horse came up lame. I naturally feel a debt of gratitude for your help.'

'Well, naturally.'

Kate added: 'And I am always upset whenever someone is hurt or killed.'

'You maybe want to keep me around to prevent your marriage to Armstrong too,' Clancy submitted playfully.

That was the wrong thing to say. Dark embers glowed within the depths of Kate's rich-chocolate-colored eyes and her sensuous lips pressed into a thin line.

'I never asked you for your help with my personal life, Mr Clancy!' She bit off each word like it left a bad taste in her mouth. 'And I refuse to be held responsible if you get yourself killed seeking vengeance for your brother's death.'

'Yes, ma'am,' he said reverently, attempting to head off her ire. 'I didn't mean to . . .'

'And you might have made a favorable impression on my little sister, but it doesn't make you my own private knight in shining armor.'

'No, ma'am.'

'Any decent human being feels remorse when an innocent man is killed.'

'Yes, ma'am.'

'Stop calling me ma'am!' Her temper flared. 'You're not talking to someone's mother!'

'No, ma'am,' he said quickly. 'I certainly don't think of you as anyone's mother.'

Kate was angrier than she should have been. She was relieved to know that Clancy was alive, more than she cared to admit. It was unsettling, confusing, disturbing. A dozen emotions were all in conflict, each seeking to overwhelm her common sense.

She found her eyes wandering to his unbuttoned shirt, aware of how the perspiration glistened on his exposed chest. Added to which his comment about her loose hair and his calling her attractive induced her heart to beat at a more rapid pace. The man's appreciative and perceptive gaze induced a feeling of warmth throughout her body and caused a shortness of breath? What was that all about?

'I'm glad you're not dead,' she stated

stiffly. Then she whirled about and returned to her horse. She had thought to climb aboard, spin the mount around and ride off in a cloud of dust, but Clancy had followed her.

'Allow me, Miss Freeman,' he offered, as she took up the reins.

Instead of waiting for her to reach for the pommel and lift her foot high enough to reach the stirrup, Clancy took hold of her waist and swung her up on to the back of the horse as if she were a child. Then he tucked her foot into the stirrup and looked to see that she had found the one on the other side. Backing up, he tipped his hat and offered an infuriatingly charming smile.

'When all the trouble is settled around here, I'd be right proud to come courting,' he said.

Kate's discomfort at having a man so unhinge her emotions almost prompted a response that he should go soak his head in a rain barrel! However, she rallied a degree of composure and simply favored him with an affirmative nod.

'Goodbye, Mr Clancy.'

'It was a pleasure seeing you again, Miss Freeman,' he responded.

Kate neck-reined the horse about and left the cemetery at an easy lope. When Clancy returned to help with the digging, York was chuckling under his breath.

'What?' Clancy wanted to know what was so funny.

'Women folk,' the oldster replied drily. 'The Lord must have certainly had himself a fun time creating such beautiful and contrary creatures. Bet he spends a good part of each day laughing at us men while we grope about in the dark. It's like he gave us a puzzle with a thousand pieces, and every piece was the same size and color. Ain't no way we mere mortals are ever going to figure out how the puzzle fits together.'

Clancy grinned. 'You could be right, York, but I sure do approve of the way those pieces look, sound and feel.'

Darren entered the house for supper with a determined set to his jaw. Stony recognized trouble, but waited until the three of them were seated. He said a short prayer in thanks for the bounty before them, then questioned his boy.

'I saw Mr Jenkins stop by the cornfield a few minutes before we quit for the day. From the grim expression on your face, I'm guessing something has happened.'

'Armstrong's men shot and killed a man today. They thought it was the guy who shot Gillum and Quint, but Mr Clancy had let some wandering cowhand borrow his horse. It was the innocent cowboy who was killed.'

Stony uttered a mild curse. 'How do we know Armstrong was behind it?'

'Cole and Flint brought in the body. They said a couple renegade Indians had shot the man for his horse.'

'Maybe that's just what happened?'

'Jenkins asked York about it before he

left town. The man had been shot by someone with a rifle, but an arrow was stuck into one of the bullet holes to lay blame on the Indians.'

'Did Mr Jenkins see Clancy?'

'No, York told him he was staying out of sight until he got word back on a telegraph message. He wouldn't say what that was about, but I'm betting Clancy has reported the killing to the US marshal's office in Denver.'

'I don't see how that will do any good. They won't send a deputy all this way for an ambush that could have been Indians.'

'I'm going to ride in and offer my help, Pa,' Darren vowed. 'If you want to argue about it, I'll remind you that Clancy saved my life.'

Rather than try to dissuade him, Stony took a helping of stew, passed the bowl to Bess and said, 'You'd best take the Sharps carbine with you. The ammo pouch has maybe twenty rounds.'

'I'm not looking to be a hero, but this

is something I have to do,' Darren reaffirmed.

'I understand, son,' Stony replied. 'If you run into more trouble than the two of you can handle, you send word and I'll recruit every farmer along the river to help.'

'You be careful,' Bess added. 'You're all the family we have left.'

Darren smiled, although it was rather pitiful with the one side of his face bruised and swollen.

8

Kate and Jenny were washing the supper dishware when Armstrong came calling. Thomas and he exchanged a simple greeting, then the man entered the kitchen. He watched as Kate passed each plate to Jenny and the younger girl used a drying towel and put the dish away in the cupboard.

'I can see Jenny has some use around the house.' The man spoke up, obviously tired of waiting for Kate to greet him.

'Jenny is helpful in a great many ways,' Kate praised her sister. 'She takes care of the pets and does much of the cleaning; she helps with the washing and tending to the horses too.'

'I spoke to your father already. I'm thinking of moving the wedding up to next month,' Armstrong declared. 'I don't see any need to put off getting married and uniting the two ranches.'

Kate stopped what she was doing and pivoted about to face the man. 'I won't be rushed off to the altar like a bride in need of a shotgun wedding,' she said firmly. 'You've never properly courted me, and there's been no formal announcement made concerning our engagement.'

The muscles in the man's face twitched and a suppressed fury glowed in the depths of his cold black eyes. The involuntary clenching of his hands into fists warned that Armstrong was a man who often resorted to physical coercion to ensure his wishes were obeyed.

'Let's not make this difficult, Kate,' he said savagely, casting civility aside. 'Your ranch is about broke. You don't have enough cattle left to pay back the loan your family owes me. You can't possibly make the next mortgage payment. If you don't marry me, this place will be on the auction block next fall.'

'You certainly know how to sway a

woman with your flattery and charm, Fulton. Is that how you managed to evade military service during the war . . . your wonderful way with words?'

The snide remark brought an instant flush of color to his complexion. When he spoke, his teeth were clenched and he hissed a malevolent threat.

'You keep up the haughty act and sass all you want.' He took a menacing step forward and the threat was thick in his voice. 'Once you're my wife, you'll learn to do what I tell you, when I tell you.'

Kate bridled at his threat. Her better judgement could not stem her dislike, resentment and suspicion of the man.

'I'm not a horse for you to buy and break to ride. And I don't intend to marry a man who would ever raise a hand to me!'

'If you renege on the wedding I'll take the ranch and everything you own. I'll send the bunch of you packing, without a penny to your name and only the clothes on your backs!'

'The wedding is off!' she exploded. 'I wouldn't marry you even if it meant living in a cave.'

He bared his tobacco-stained teeth in a sneer. 'Then you'll damn well end up begging on the streets — you and your dim-witted sister both!'

'Get out of our house!' Kate shouted hotly. 'Your wicked and evil days are numbered. We know you had Jocko kill Choctaw and steal our cattle!'

Rather than display surprise, Armstrong guffawed his contempt. 'Your pal Clancy is dead. Any far-fetched rumors he might have started died with him.'

'You and your bungling bunch of hired idiots didn't kill Clancy; you killed an innocent cowhand. Clancy is gathering evidence right now that is going to put a rope around your neck!'

The words were out before she could stop them. Kate realized the error at once, but it was too late to take back her words. Armstrong scowled in confusion, then muttered a shocked, 'Clancy is still alive?'

Kate didn't reply this time. She ducked her head to hide her consternation at being so foolish. Her defensive anger had put Clancy's life at risk.

Armstrong didn't make any more threats. He pivoted about and marched smartly out of the house.

'Dear Lord!' Kate exclaimed. 'What have I done?'

★   ★   ★

'Son,' York spoke to Clancy, 'I don't know why you want to wash off all of your body's natural protection by taking a bath.'

'I worked up quite a sweat burying Johnson, and I've not had a decent bath in a week.'

'Man shouldn't worry about bathing, less'n he's getting married or going to visit his ma. Shucks, I don't do more than rinse off once a month, and even then it leaves me feeling exposed and vulnerable to miseries.'

Clancy had the water in the tub — it

147

was actually a small, oval, watering trough that wasn't in use — and he had his one change of clothes laid out on a bale of straw. He removed his shirt and had his hands on his waistband when a man appeared at the barn entrance.

'Mr York?' Darren Baker called out. 'That you back in the shadows?'

'I'm here . . . the one with his clothes on and his brain working. I can't say the same for this other joker.'

Darren walked through the barn until he could make out Clancy and the tub of water. He stopped and grinned . . . or presented what looked like a grin.

'You going courting?' he asked.

'I'm going to wash off a layer of dust and grime,' Clancy replied. 'At least, that was my intention when I heated water to fill this trough.'

'I won't keep you from the chore,' Darren assured him. 'I only stopped by to offer my help.'

'Why would I need your help?'

'Armstrong has a half-dozen gunmen

on his payroll. That's a lot for one man to handle.'

'Don't be counting Jocko as one of them,' York put in. 'Clancy kilt him over in Kansas City.'

'Jocko's dead?' Darren didn't hide his surprise. 'How did you come to kill Jocko?'

'He interrupted me when I was about to take a bath and the water got cold,' Clancy growled. 'Speak your mind, Baker.'

Darren chuckled. 'I just wanted you to know that I've got a rifle and I'm a passable shot. I'm here to lend a hand, if you've a mind to take on Armstrong and his bunch.'

York teased: 'There you are, Clancy. I was worried that I'd be your only help, and I'm about as blind as a gopher if a target is beyond a hundred feet. At least Darren's got good eyesight.'

'Tell you what,' Clancy told Darren. 'I'm waiting on word from the law about Armstrong. If a warrant is issued for his arrest, I intend to take him in. If his men decide to take his side against the law, I might be forced to recruit a few men. It would be a real help to know how many are willing to join a posse.'

'You sound like a lawman.'

'Only if the marshal's office issues a warrant. Otherwise, it's personal.'

'That's good enough for me,' Darren said. 'Counting the boys over sixteen and the able-bodied men, we've got six or seven farmers who might join. Around town, we might get another four or five. The problem is, some of them have never done much fighting.'

'Soon as I hear back from the marshal's office, I'll let you know my plan,' Clancy promised. 'You can put those who are willing on alert and be ready. York will contact you when and if the need arises.'

'I'll pass the word, Mr Clancy. You can count on me.'

Clancy watched him leave and looked over at York. 'Take a look after the boy and see if anyone is following him or showing a little too much interest.'

'I got what you mean,' York replied. Then he hurried after Darren so he would be in a position to watch him leave town.

No sooner had Darren disappeared down the road than a second rider came up to the livery. York was curious on seeing Kate arrive on a lathered up pony. He was even more surprised at the way she jumped down from her horse and ran up to him.

'Where's Mr Clancy?' she asked, panting from being out of breath. 'I've got to see him!'

York hesitated before answering. 'Wa'al, Miss Kate, he's in the barn,' he said carefully. Then added: 'But he ain't exactly in the best of shape for visitors.'

She gasped. 'He's been hurt! You should have sent someone for me!'

'Easy gal, don't get your bloomers tangled,' York began to explain. 'It ain't what you think.'

But Kate rushed past him, fearful,

dreading what might have happened. York called after her, but she had to see Clancy for herself and know that he was all right.

Charging through the barn at breakneck speed, Kate made out something in the shadows at the far end of the shelter. It looked as if a small bed had been placed in the middle of the room. The man's upper body was visible in the gloom, so it appeared that Clancy was able to sit up.

Now a person's body usually does what the brain tells it to, but there are times when the brain's response is a whole lot quicker than the body's. Kate's legs were pumping furiously, as she was running hard from an inexpressible concern and trepidation. At last her eyes finally penetrated the darkness enough for her to make out Clancy, and he was sitting in a tub . . . taking a bath!

Kate's brain abruptly wailed: *Whoa! Stop! Right now!*

But her legs were going much too

fast. She applied brakes in mid-sprint and skidded on the straw-strewn barn floor. Both feet flew out from under her and she landed in a clumsy, half-sitting, half lying on her back, position, and slid about fifteen feet. Such an ungainly approach caused her dress to ride up until it bunched at her waist. By the time her body stopped its precarious slide, she was ten feet from the tub and Clancy was staring at her with eyes wide and mouth agape.

Quickly pulling her skirt down to her ankles, Kate scrambled to her feet, mumbled a hasty 'Excuse me!' and dashed back to the barn entrance.

York was grinning like a prankster, trying hard not to laugh. However, one glimpse of Kate's expression of ire and humiliation removed any notion of amusement.

'Why didn't you tell me Mr Clancy was taking a bath?' she demanded.

York swallowed the last trace of humor and held up both hands, palms outward, ready to ward off blows should the girl start swinging her fists at him.

'I was getting to it, Miss Freeman,' he lamented weakly. 'You done flew past me before I could give you the details.'

In order to control both her anger and embarrassment, Kate began to dust off the back of her dress. 'I'm going to smell like a stable,' she said bitterly. 'Don't you ever sweep or clean your floor?'

'My animals are much less particular than female folks when it comes to complaining about a little dirt or horse ... ' He struggled for a polite word and finished with, '. . . uh, horse leavings.'

'I don't know how Granny puts up with you,' Kate said tersely. 'And it's no wonder why you never married.'

York was immediately defensive. 'The main reason I never got married is because I never asked no troublesome female for her hand.'

Kate scowled at him. 'At least, you were saved the letdown of having each and every one of them say no.'

Fearful of why the girl had made a ride at dusk, Clancy hurriedly toweled himself off and dressed. As he joined the pair at the front of the barn, York was saying something about women critters being a curse to mankind.

Kate looked ready for a heated riposte, but withheld her retort at his approach. He attempted to dismiss their verbal jousting with a smile of greeting.

'Miss Freeman, what brings you into town so late?'

Visibly thankful that he made no mention of her abrupt intrusion upon his bath, Kate told him about her exchange with Armstrong and how she had inadvertently told him that the man killed in the ambush was a stranger looking for a job.

'Now he knows you're still alive.' York voiced the obvious.

'More than that,' Kate confessed. 'I told him you knew about our cattle being stolen and that you were working to find evidence to prove it.'

'What'd I tell you, Clancy?' York barked sourly. 'You gotta always keep your mouth shut around a woman.'

'I let him goad me into it,' Kate apologized. 'When he threatened to teach me a lesson in obedience once we were married, I . . . ' She waved her hand in a sign of defeat.

York looked back at Clancy. 'That means you'll need to watch your back, son, even while you're here in town. If Armstrong thinks you might prove he killed Choctaw and stole the Freeman herd, he'll have to shut you up quick.'

'I'm so sorry,' Kate said.

Clancy reached out and patted her on the shoulder. 'Don't worry about it. I was going to ride up and confront him tomorrow anyway.'

'Yeah, but now he'll be ready for you,' York pointed out. 'You've lost the edge of surprise.'

Clancy ignored York's pessimism and directed his words at Kate. 'It's going to be late by the time you get home. With

Armstrong alerted, it isn't safe to ride the road to your place after dark.'

'There is a back way I can take that will be safe.'

Clancy didn't like that idea. 'I'll take you home. You can borrow one of York's rental nags and leave your lathered-up horse here for the night.'

The girl bridled at the offer. 'I don't need someone to watch over me. I know my way through the hills.'

'I'm not willing to take that chance,' Clancy responded. 'With Armstrong knowing why I'm here, I need to find a way to stay one step ahead.'

York snorted. 'About the only one you're going to be one step ahead of is the devil. I'm gonna fix you a nice coffin for the next time I see you.'

9

Ringer arrived for the evening meal, which Armstrong's cook had prepared, and immediately took note of the man's controlled fury.

'What's the matter, boss?' he asked. 'I thought you'd be all smiles tonight.'

'The man Cole and Flint killed today was a wandering cowpoke looking for work. Clancy acted the good Samaritan and loaned the fellow his horse. He was on his way here to ask about a job!'

Ringer swore. 'That's going to make things a little more interesting.'

'Interesting ain't the half of it,' Armstrong grumbled. 'According to my ex-bride-to-be the man is rounding up evidence to show that we stole their herd of cattle and killed Choctaw.'

'What?' Ringer did not hide his

shock. 'How in the dickens could he know about that?'

'I don't know. Maybe he was in Kansas City when the herd was sold. Or he might have been around when Jocko was killed and heard something.'

'Clancy is smart enough to have managed to follow us all the way from Andersonville; he will sure enough link us to the rustling and murder,' Ringer asserted. 'We've got to kill that man, and I mean like right now!'

'Soon as we eat, you take Flint and Cole into town. I'll ride over to the line shack and bring Arno and Wart back here. Until we deal with Clancy, we stay ready with three men looking for him and three of us waiting and watching for him here.'

'What if he contacted the law?' Ringer asked.

'It won't matter. We can claim he got killed in a dispute over a woman, or he bullied one of our men into a gunfight. The law ain't going to be interested in anything going on this far from a major city. Clancy's investigation will come to an abrupt end as soon as the man takes his last breath.'

* * *

Clancy and Kate rode in relative silence along the dark path. The way had once been a road of sorts, but the main route was much easier for a wagon. This trail was overgrown and difficult to follow at times. When they reached a plateau, Kate pulled back on her reins enough to fall in alongside Clancy.

'You didn't have to accompany me,' she said, opening the conversation. 'Few Indians ever stray this far.'

'It didn't feel right,' he answered back. 'A beautiful young woman shouldn't be riding at night by herself.'

'Why is finding this sergeant so important to you?' she asked. 'You said that thousands of men died in Andersonville. That means any number of guards might have been responsible for your brother's death.'

160

'Jeff wore our mother's wedding ring around his neck,' Clancy told her. 'It was his lucky charm . . . or so he liked to say.'

'And you think Sergeant Fuller stole it?'

'Jeffrey didn't go to war because he thought it was right.' Clancy didn't answer her question. 'He went because I did. We joined up together, we were in the same outfit, we billeted together and suffered from the cold, the heat, the bad food and water together. I was responsible for him.

'Even as kids, Jeff would follow me everywhere. He wasn't an ambitious kid, but he would often help me when I was working, just because he liked to be with me. When our folks died he looked to me for support and direction. I left a good job to join up and fight for the Union. Neither of us had ever seen a slave, but I didn't like the notion of anyone enslaving anyone else. Jeff came along because I went, not because of his own feelings about the

Union or the Confederacy.'

'How did he end up in Andersonville?' Kate asked.

'We got separated. I volunteered for a patrol, but Jeff was worn out and wanted to get some extra rest. He should have been safe in camp, except there was a sneak attack by a Confederate outfit while we were off scouting in a different direction. By the time we got back to camp it had been wiped out. We found a few stragglers and some who were too wounded to walk — that was all the Johnny Rebs left behind. My brother was captured and I wasn't there to protect him.'

'You talk like your brother was more like a son. How old was he?'

'Five years younger than me, twenty-two when he was captured.'

'That's not exactly a child.'

'No, but Jeff was always dependent on me. He was . . . well, a lot weaker than I was at that age. He didn't like to make decisions or take responsibility. I hoped the war would make a man of him, but it only got him killed.'

'I'm sorry,' Kate said gently.

'How about you?' Clancy changed the subject. 'You're a right special lady to still be without a husband. With the number of men compared to the few eligible women available, it's a real puzzle that you're still unattached.'

Kate hesitated and he thought, for a moment, that she would not answer. He was about to quash the question, when she began to speak.

'I haven't lacked for suitors, Mr Clancy. But my mother died giving birth to Jenny. As you pointed out concerning her condition, Jenny was born after my mother had thought she was too old to have any more children. My father was fifteen years older than Mom, so they were both well along in years.

'When Jenny arrived I became responsible for her. I raised her as best I could and I've had to be more than her big sister. I'm her caretaker, the one responsible for looking after her.'

163

'And most of your suitors didn't want a child around that will never mature.'

'Exactly.'

'Speaking for myself, I found Jenny to be very sweet.'

The trail began to narrow so Kate moved her horse to the lead again. That was the end of their dialog, because of the heavy growth of brush and trees. The path was sinuous and steep, making conversation impossible. However, Kate felt a tingle of apprehension. Here was a man who wasn't discouraged at the thought of having Jenny around. Moreover, he had said he wanted to court her.

Slow down, my beating heart, she scolded herself. Clancy has to survive his conflict with Armstrong before I start having romantic notions about him.

* * *

Ringer and his two men tied off their horses at the saloon hitching post. 'You check around town, Cole,' Ringer told the one hired hand. 'See if there's anything going on we ought to know about. Flint and I will go talk to York.'

Flint was at Ringer's side as they walked down to the livery. As they approached the barn, he said, 'Frosty York is an ornery sort, Ringer. How far does the boss want us to take this?'

'We'll be polite unless he needs some persuading to cooperate,' Ringer assured Flint. 'York ain't such a fool as to go against us.'

'What about his in-law crone, the one who runs the office?'

'She ought to be in bed by this time. We won't have any trouble with her.'

They heard the pounding of a hammer on metal and turned toward the blacksmith side of the livery. The forge glowed hot and the bellows were covered in soot. York was holding a large hammer and a piece of metal he had just beaten flat on the anvil. He paused from his inspection at the approach of the two men.

'We've a couple questions for you, York,' Ringer announced haughtily. 'You be straight with us and we'll be out of your hair in two minutes.'

York set down the metal strip and turned to confront them.

'What's on your mind, Ringer?' the old boy asked.

'We're looking for Clancy.' Flint was the one to reply. 'He gave you some boneyard business when he killed our two friends, Gillum and Quint.'

'I do a lot of different jobs, children.' Purposely he spoke down to them. 'But I ain't in charge of keeping track of every sodbuster or drifter who wanders into town.'

Ringer and Flint moved within arm's length. Ringer was the one to speak this time. 'We don't want to hurt you, old man. Get rid of the hammer and tell us what Clancy has been doing. Who he has been sending telegraph messages to? Answer me, and we'll let you stay in one piece.'

York raised his hands up to shoulder

166

height, as if to surrender. Instead, he pitched down the heavy hammer . . . right on Flint's foot!

Flint cried out from the pain, but his wail of anguish was silenced when York slammed him alongside the jaw with a rock hard fist. By the time he hit the floor, York had Ringer by the throat, his grip like a vice, his muscular arms hard from his blacksmithing work.

Ringer grabbed York's wrists, gasping for air. York whirled him about like a rag doll and shoved him back against the forge. A blazing hot fire scorched Ringer's backside and he cried out in pain. With the ease of tossing around a sack of grain, York picked Ringer up and physically sat him in his bucket of cooling water.

'Warn me again about what you're gonna do to me, sonny boy.' York snarled the words, his face about two inches from Ringer's own. 'You two tough *hombres* about skeered me to death!'

Tears ran down Ringer's scarlet face.

He was terrified that York would sit him once more on the white-hot embers of his forge. Unable to form any words, he shook his head vigorously from side to side.

York snorted his contempt, removed Ringer's gun from its holster, and threw him to the ground. Then he bent over Flint and took his gun. He tossed both weapons into his water bucket.

'You got any more questions to ask?' he challenged Ringer, standing over them like a grim reaper, ready to extinguish both of their lives.

Without a word Ringer quickly helped Flint to his feet. Then, still sobbing from humiliation, Ringer about ran from the barn.

'It's a crying shame,' York muttered after them. 'God just ain't turning out men like he used to. Most of them are a bunch of damn pansies these days.'

Flint hobbled along with Ringer's help, still half woozy from York's vicious punch. They reached their horses as Cole came out of the saloon.

'Might be something going on,' Cole said, before he had a good look at Ringer and Flint.

'What's that?' Ringer asked, blinking to hide the last of his tears.

'Holy Hanna! What happened to Flint?'

'He's got a couple of smashed toes and York socked him a good one.'

'You look shaken up, too.'

Ringer hated the hot flush in his face. He was glad it was dark enough to hide his shame. 'The old coot knocked me up against his forge. I'm going to have some blisters that are going to make riding a real discomfort.'

'Did you work him over?'

'He took us by surprise,' Ringer said lamely. 'But he told us enough. What did you find out?'

'The Bakers have been in town and talked to Clancy. There's a good chance the farmers are going to back his play.'

'We better get back. If Clancy isn't in town he must be recruiting help. We need to be ready for anything.'

'Clancy left town with the Freeman girl. She arrived around dusk and they left by way of the old road.'

Ringer considered the news. 'Then he'll be at their place tonight.'

'Can you ride a horse?' Cole asked Flint.

Flint groaned, his brain still in a thick fog. 'Mebbe.' His words were slurred. 'Jus' don't put me on the nag what done kicked me in the face!'

'Help me get him on his horse,' Ringer said. 'If need be, we'll tie him on. We need to get back to the ranch.'

York had kept to the shadows and followed along. He heard the three men discussing the situation and knew Clancy would have no chance against such long odds. He waited until the riders were out of sight, before he headed back for the barn. Things were heating up right quick. If someone in town had seen him and the girl ride out . . .

'I knew that fella was trouble on the

hoof,' he said aloud. 'I reckon there's only one thing for me to do.'

* * *

Clancy and Kate put the two horses into the small holding corral. There was water and some cut wild grass in a manger, but Clancy also gave each of them a handful of oats.

'You carry grain with you?' Kate asked.

'It doesn't hurt to spoil an animal when you might need him to save your life. Nugget has been through a long few months. We've traveled several thousand miles together in the past year and he's never let me down.'

'You're not going to ride over to Armstrong's place alone tomorrow?'

'I've proof he stole your cattle. The brand inspector had one of the steers butchered so they would have the evidence needed. As you probably know, when looking at the inside of a cow's hide, it's easy to see when a running iron has been used to alter a brand.'

171

'How does that prove anything against Armstrong? You said it was Jocko who sold the cattle.'

'Yes, but he put the money from the sale into the bank under Armstrong's name. I requested a judge to issue a freeze on that account until you got your money back.'

It was dark, except for a half moon in the night sky, but Clancy could tell that the lady was impressed. Surprised and impressed. Instead of thanking him for his efforts or saying something flattering about his handling of the situation, the girl shook her head.

'You'll be dead by tomorrow night. Then we'll be right back where we were before you arrived.'

'I've been in a few battles, Miss Freeman. And I've got right on my side.'

Rather than carry forward that discussion, Kate gestured toward a building a short distance from the house.

'You can spend the night in the bunkhouse. Our two men are scouring the hills for what few beef we have left. You ought to be safe for one night.'

'Thank you.'

'Breakfast is usually ready at sunup. Will that work for you?'

'I won't be here. I need to be in a position to keep watch over the Armstrong ranch. You did say it was a mile west of here?'

'The trail begins along the base of the ridge beyond the corrals. It's fairly well worn, but there isn't much cover in some places.'

'I'll be fine.'

Kate uttered a sigh of resignation. 'No,' she murmured back. 'No, you won't.'

'Goodnight, Miss Freeman,' Clancy said, unable to think of anything else.

The girl's shoulders were bowed a little, not nearly so erect as usual, as she walked toward the house. Clancy knew how she must be feeling. He had arrived on the scene like the proverbial hero, out to save her ranch and arrest the man responsible for murdering her hired hand and stealing her cattle. Now, confronted with the reality of the situation, Clancy was alone and mightily outgunned. Kate surely assumed all would be lost.

With a sigh of resignation, Clancy rounded up his gear and entered the bunkhouse. There were four beds in the room, all empty. He took one next to the wall and sank down for a few hours' rest. Setting his mental alarm for daylight, he lay back and wondered if this would be the last night of his life.

★ ★ ★

'You're going to get yourself shot full of holes!' Granny warned York. 'How am I supposed to run the way station, the telegraph, do the post and handle all of the work at the livery too?'

'The boy is in over his head, Gran,' York told her. 'If I don't get the farmers to help, that young man will be dead before the sun sets tomorrow.'

'And how is your also being dead going to help?'

York allowed a softness to enter his face, something very rare for him. 'Listen to me, Gran,' he said gently. 'I know I've never said thank you for all the help you've given me here. I suspect I've even commented a few times that you were troublesome to have around. But we are family . . . the only family either of us got left. You never met a man you could live with, and I never met a woman I could live with. Yet, you and me have gotten by passably by dividing the work and sharing what we had.'

'You've been very good to me,' Granny offered back. 'And . . . I care about you, about your safety.'

'Every man has his responsibilities, Gran,' York explained. 'A man don't mistreat a woman, he does an honest day's work, and he stands up for what's right. We don't have a lawman around here, so we have to join together and see that justice is served.'

Granny relaxed her posture and her voice revealed her affection. 'Cantankerous old coot that you are, you've got a good heart.'

'Bothersome, nagging female that you are, I'm used to having you around,' York replied, also allowing the fondness to enter his voice.

The elderly woman smiled. 'Be careful, Frosty.'

'Go to bed and don't worry, Gran. I'll likely be back by the time you get up.'

* * *

Ringer stormed through the door and tossed his hat on the table. Before speaking to Armstrong, he went to the liquor cabinet and poured himself a drink.

'Well?' Armstrong asked impatiently. 'Talk to me.'

Ringer gulped down several swallows of whiskey. It burned his throat and his eyes watered, but he grit his teeth and took another drink before speaking.

'The cat has clawed its way out of the bag, boss. Clancy is over at the Freeman place — or should be by this time. We got to town and learned he had left with Kate Freeman.'

'What about York?'

'The old wart hit Flint on the foot with a hammer and about set fire to my britches. He's tougher than a razorback boar.'

Armstrong shook his head. 'How's Flint?'

'Smashed his toes somewhat, but they don't appear broken. He's soaking his foot in some hot water.'

'So Clancy has taken up with the Freemans?' Armstrong was thoughtful. 'That means he will have told them everything.'

'They will sure enough send for a deputy US marshal or something.'

Armstrong rubbed his hands together. 'Then we'll make sure there is no one left to point a finger at us.'

'What's your idea?' Ringer wanted to know.

'Have the boys saddle up . . . including Flint. We're going to pay a visit to our neighbors.'

'You mean tonight?'

'Clancy has declared war against us and I'm sick and tired of him dictating the rules. We have to act quickly and decisively or we'll lose everything.'

'I'll get the boys armed and mounted up,' Ringer vowed.

'Get a horse ready for me too. I need to round up a couple of things for our visit. I'll meet you and the boys in the yard.'

10

Kate had been unable to sleep. She went over a hundred scenarios in her head about Clancy taking on Armstrong and his gang. None of them worked out in his favor. The odds were too great.

She pictured the man in her mind and could not help feeling an attraction for him. He was an honorable man, with a desire for justice. He had killed three of Armstrong's men, yet there was an innate gentleness about him. The way he treated Jenny was the same as her father had done, showing her the respect due to a woman, yet able to relate to her as a child. What an odd combination for a man.

Then there was the way he looked at her, as if she was special, with a subdued yearning in his eyes. Given a chance, she knew they would become more than friends. He was the kind of man she had been waiting for, a man who would not only love her, but would accept Jenny as a part of their lives.

Too bad he's going to die tomorrow, she thought. *We could have been . . .*

There came the sound of footsteps!

Kate jumped to her feet and grabbed her robe. She barely managed to pull it on before a match flared in the main room. By the time a lamp was lit, three men were moving through the house!

'Jenny!' Kate woke up her sister, while quickly closing the bedroom door. 'Jenny, you must hide!'

The girl sat up, frightened. 'What's wrong, Kate?'

'You know the secret place, the one I've showed you?' At Jenny's nod, she hurried to grab up a blanket. 'You must go there right now!'

'Is it Indians?' Jenny asked.

'Worse than that,' Kate replied. 'You go there and stay hidden. Don't make a sound until I come for you.'

Jenny hurried to do as she was told.

180

In order to cover her sister's escape, Kate went out of the bedroom, hurrying to reach her father.

'There you are!' Armstrong's bass voice sounded in triumph. 'Come in, Kate, and sit down.'

Shakes began to bark, but one of the men silenced him with a swift boot to his rear. He ran out of the open front door to lick his bruise.

'What's the meaning of this?' Kate demanded to know. 'You've got more brass than brains, entering our house uninvited.'

Flint was out on the porch, keeping watch. Arno and Cole escorted Tom into the room. Once he was seated in his usual chair, Armstrong used his gun as a pointer and waved to Cole.

'Have Ringer cover you and Wart, while you bring in our guest from the bunkhouse. Arno, you check the house for weapons.'

'Fulton,' Tom cried, 'Are you out of your mind?'

'Just sit tight and shut your mouth,

old man.' Armstrong paused and looked around. 'Where's the dummy?'

'Jenny is not a dummy!' Kate defended her sister.

'Flint, take a look in the bedroom.'

Hobbling mostly on one foot, Flint went into the girl's room. He threw open the door and looked around. 'She ain't here,' he announced. 'Window is open, so she must have slipped out.'

'You'll never find her,' Kate said smugly. 'Jenny is very good at hiding.'

There came the sound of voices beyond the door and Armstrong waited, gun in hand, until Morgan Clancy was herded into the room.

'Gave up without a fight,' said Cole. 'Soon as we told him we had the woman and her pa, he come along gentle as a lamb.'

'You have his gun?'

'I left his rig on the porch, like you said. It will look as if he had it with him when they sort through the debris.'

Clancy glanced at Kate and Tom, then pinned Armstrong with a cold stare. 'You're Sergeant Fuller,' he said. 'You're responsible for the deaths of hundreds of men, including my brother.'

'It was war, Clancy,' Armstrong said, shrugging it off. 'Captain Wirz said to make sure none of the Yankee prisoners ever took up arms against the Confederacy again.' He grunted. 'Well, none of them ever did.'

'You're the lowest form of vermin, Fuller,' Clancy said. 'If I don't get a chance to make you pay, God will serve up a punishment befitting your crimes.'

Armstrong guffawed his disdain. 'After all of the killing and brutality of war, do you really think God will be interested in me?'

Clancy didn't answer because another of Armstrong's men entered.

'We finished a search of the place. Clancy was the only one using the bunkhouse.'

'Owens and Ingersoll are gathering beef,' Tom told the intruders. He added coldly, 'The few that you left us.'

183

'I never meant you any harm, Freeman,' Armstrong informed him. 'If Kate and me had wed, the two ranches would have been combined. Everything would have turned out fine.'

'Except for you killing Choctaw and stealing a hundred head of their cattle,' Clancy put in. 'That isn't exactly the way you win a lady's hand.'

'It's exactly the way,' Armstrong jeered his reply. 'But things took a downward turn when you showed up. What happens next is all on you, Clancy.'

'I've been acting on behalf of the US marshal's office, Fuller. The marshal himself will come after you if you kill me.'

'I'll take that chance,' Armstrong said. 'Once all of you are found in the ashes, there won't be any questions except to wonder how the fire started.'

Two more men entered the room. They were carrying lengths of rope.

'Cole, you and Wart tie up our three guests. Arno, tell Ringer that Jenny escaped. You two see if you can find her.' Arno left and Armstrong instructed the others. 'Flint, keep a gun on these three while they are properly bound up. I'm going to prepare a little house-warming party for them all.'

Tom was the first to be secured in his chair by a length of rope. Next Clancy and Kate were tied up and sat down on the couch.

'Good job,' Flint told the two men. 'It's only got to hold them for five minutes. After that . . . ' He didn't finish and Wart and Cole left the room.

'Too bad it wasn't you we killed on the trail,' Flint taunted Clancy. 'There would have been no need for this.'

'You're as bad as Sergeant Fuller,' Clancy said. 'Lowest scum to ever walk the earth on his hind legs.'

'It was war,' Flint maintained. 'We all did what we had to in order to survive. As for the fleecing of the Yanks, that was the only way to come out of the war ahead.'

'You needn't look for Jenny,' Kate

said. 'She isn't any threat to you. She won't be able to tell anyone about this.'

'Not my call, Miss Freeman.' Flint started toward the door and hesitated, looking back at her. 'I'm sorry you learned the truth. I ain't never killed a woman before.'

'That's one worse level of hell you'll go to after you die,' Clancy promised.

Flint went out without further comment and closed the door.

After a few moments there was activity along the front of the house. It sounded like men with buckets, splashing the walls.

'I smell coal oil,' Tom said. 'They are going to set fire to the house.'

Clancy worked mightily against the ropes, but Armstrong's men had done a good job. The place would soon be a blazing inferno and the three of them were sure to perish.

'I'm damn sorry for causing all this.' Clancy spoke to Tom. 'If I hadn't come to town, you and your daughters would be safe.'

'It wouldn't have been for long,' Tom replied. 'Armstrong would have taken over our ranch. He would have been a rotten husband to Kate and he would have shipped Jenny off to an asylum. I recognized him for what he was, but I was too old to fight, and a cripple to boot. I couldn't stand up to him.'

'And I would rather die with the two of you than be married to a monster like Armstrong,' Kate asserted. 'He didn't even deny your claims about his war crimes.'

Clancy turned and stared into Kate's eyes. They were bright, shining with fear and restrained tears, yet there was something else.

'As I'll never get the chance to say it again, Miss Freeman,' Clancy said softly. 'I'm pretty sure I'm in love with you.'

'We've only been together for a few hours,' Kate objected. 'How can you think you love me?'

'What's not to love?' Clancy retorted. 'You're warm and charming and the

187

prettiest gal I ever set eyes on. If I had the time to do it proper, I'd sure enough come courting and try to win your hand.'

Boldly, Kate smiled at his declaration. 'As we are about to be roasted alive, I'll come right out and admit I would very much enjoy having you come courting.'

Clancy leaned toward her and was rewarded by her inclining his direction. It was awkward and tentative, but they managed a single kiss.

'There she goes!' Tom gasped his horror. 'They've set fire to the house.'

Clancy glanced at the window and saw flames engulfing the front of the building. He whispered over the crackling of the flames. 'If only we had more time.'

'Yes,' Kate murmured back. 'I would have loved to have you hold me in your arms.'

The heat seared the exterior of the house and the glass in the windows shattered. The fire spread rapidly, engulfing the roof and attacking the curtains. Nothing could prevent the total destruction of the Freeman ranch house.

*   *   *

'Look at that!' Darren shouted, pointing up the hill to the bright glow. 'The Big Diamond ranch is on fire!'

'We're too late!' York cried. 'Come on, men. We're out of time!'

The six riders risked the lives of themselves and their horses, galloping along the dark trail. York had thought they would arrive in time to ride along with Clancy. With several guns, they might have had a chance against Armstrong. Now, with the orange radiance of a raging fire against the night sky, he feared they would be too late to offer any real help. Instead of a rescue party, they were going to be a burial party.

*   *   *

Suddenly, confined in the living room, practically smothered by the heat and smoke, a shadow appeared.

'Jenny!' Kate cried. 'You must get out of here!'

But Jenny hurried over to Clancy. 'I sneaked up and got your gun,' she told him, holding out the revolver. 'The men were all looking for Jenny, but I was under the porch and didn't let them see me.'

'Good girl,' Clancy praised. 'Can you untie me?'

Jenny cast a fearful look at the fire. The front of the house was a wall of flame. Time was running out.

'Hurry, Jenny,' he coaxed. 'Just undo the one big knot and we'll get out the back way.'

Jenny put the gun down and began to work furiously on the rope. She tugged and pulled and at last he came free.

'Untie your father,' Clancy told her, sticking the gun into his belt, 'while I get these ropes off Kate.'

'Ooh,' Jenny cried, covering her head

with both hands. 'It's getting real hot.'

Cinders were spilling from the ceiling and the roof and walls were about to come down. Clancy jumped over and jerked the knot free to release Tom. 'Get going!' he shouted over the roar of the fire. 'I'll bring Kate.'

Jenny and Tom hurried through the girl's bedroom, while Clancy lifted Kate up into his arms. Ash sprinkled down his neck and the ceiling beams were ablaze. The furnace-like heat scorched his bare skin and smoke burned his eyes, as he carried Kate out of the room. Even as he went through the bedroom door the roof caved in on the main sitting room.

Jenny and Tom were already climbing out of the back window. Clancy got there and passed Kate to Tom. As he worked to untie her, Clancy followed them through the opening. He pulled his gun and searched for an escape route.

'They can't see you if you follow Jenny,' the girl spoke up.

'Lead the way,' Clancy told her. 'We'll be right behind you.'

Jenny went directly back of the house and entered a run-off ditch. Then she turned and worked back, round to the rear of the bunkhouse. It had caught fire from the flying ashes from the house, but the animals were safe. The barn was well away from the fire.

Clancy could see Armstrong and his men scattered about out front, watching the burning structures that lit up the entire yard.

'Hey!' a voice called out from a short way off. 'There goes the girl!'

The man started forward at a run, certain the shadow he had seen hurrying toward the ditch was Jenny. By the time he spotted Clancy and the others, he was only fifty feet away.

Clancy stopped, took aim, and fired before the man could get his gun out. It took two shots to put him down, but he collapsed without calling a warning or getting off a shot of his own.

'The girl must have a gun!' cried a

voice that sounded like Arno. Clancy saw a second figure come into the light, a short distance away. The man shouted: 'She just shot Wart!'

'You three take that side!' Armstrong bellowed the command. 'Ringer, you and I will cover the other.'

'I can see Clancy's holster on the porch,' Flint called out. 'His gun is missing. Jenny must have grabbed the pistol while we were searching the hills.'

'One gun won't last her for long,' a man said. 'I can't believe she got Wart!'

Clancy followed the others to a shallow wash. As he looked back, Arno was checking on the downed man.

'Durn lucky shooting,' he said. 'Wart's done for.'

Clancy took a position at the top of the ditch, while Jenny, Kate and Tom all huddled below him, protected by the depth of the wash. It was not a great place to defend, being open to either side for fifty feet or more, but it would have to do.

Three shadows approached with

guns out, partly hidden by the smoke and darkness. Clancy chose the closest target, took careful aim and fired.

The man yelped, struck by the bullet and fell to his knees. The other two men dove for cover.

'Arno!' one of them yelled. 'You hit bad?'

'I'm out of the fight,' Arno replied. 'The bullet hit me in the hip. I don't think I can walk.'

Cole directed, 'You keep to cover. Flint and I will get that little wildcat.'

'Whod'a thunk the kid could shoot thataway?' Flint said in amazement.

'She's only got one or two bullets left,' Cole said. 'Keep low and don't give her a target to shoot at.'

Armstrong and Ringer had reached the other side. They managed to save the chaise from the burning flames and were pushing it along the open ground, using it for cover.

'Where's she at?' Armstrong called out to his men.

'The shot came from the gully at the

base of the hill,' Cole yelled back. 'Can't get a shot at her from here.'

'We'll use the buggy for cover and close in. If we flush her out, you boys knock her down. We need for her body to be burned in the house with the others.'

Cole and Flint were crawling toward the ditch. Once at the wash they could move to a point where they would have an open field of fire at Clancy. As the wash bellied out to the other side, there wasn't enough cover to get past the buggy in that direction. Time was running out.

11

'That's gunfire,' Darren said to York. 'The Freemans are still putting up a fight.'

'All right, boys,' York outlined. 'Soon as we hit the yard, we break up into two teams. Stick together so we don't end up shooting at each other. Me and the Collin boys will go to the right side of the main house and handle any of Armstrong's men on that side. Darren, you and your pa take Jenkins and go to the left. If they're burning the place down, Armstrong must intend to kill everyone in the family, along with Clancy.'

'We hear you,' Darren said tightly. 'If we have to, we shoot to kill.'

'It's just at the top of this hill,' Stony warned. 'Everyone be ready.'

$\star$ $\star$ $\star$

Clancy fired a shot at Armstrong, but the bullet struck the side of the chaise. He cursed the waste of the round and ducked back down.

Searching for a route that would allow the others to escape or hide, there was nothing for a hundred feet up the hill. To try and climb to safety would have been futile, as well as suicidal, unless . . . ?

'When I tell you to run, you three head up the hill. If you can reach the trees, you'll have cover and a chance to hide or get away.'

'Be sensible, son,' Tom said. 'I can't walk more than a few steps. Give me the gun and I'll cover you and the girls. Maybe you can get them to safety.'

Clancy knew the man was telling the truth, but Kate would never leave his side, even if it meant a chance for her and Jenny to escape. He had no options but to make a final stand and try to kill them all.

Abruptly, the night was split with gunfire and men shouted in confusion.

Flint and Cole broke for their horses, but two groups of riders cut them off.

Armstrong and Ringer were too far from their mounts. They had only one escape path . . . directly past Clancy's position.

'We kill that girl and no one can say this wasn't an Indian raiding party,' Armstrong shouted to Ringer. 'We can say we saw the fire and came to drive them off.'

'But the posse will hear us shooting.'

Armstrong outlined the story. 'Jenny is a child. She didn't know we came to help and she shot at us. Before we could get to her, the Indians shot and killed her.'

'I'm with you,' Ringer said. 'The girl's fired at least five shots, so she either has one left or she's empty.'

'We have to hurry, or the men might break down and talk,' Armstrong said.

'You're the boss.'

'Keep moving and she won't be able to get a bead on us. If we can make her miss her last shot, we'll finish with her, then head up into the hills and circle back to the ranch. We'll say we ran off the last of the renegades, after one of them shot Jenny. That will explain everything.'

Clancy saw the two phantoms coming towards his position. They ran a zigzag pattern, trying to get close enough for a clear shot.

Clancy fired once and missed. He couldn't afford any more mistakes and they were getting too close. A stray shot could hit the three people huddled in the shadows below him. Fear for their safety prompted him to climb up from his hiding-place and brazenly take on the two men.

'That's close enough!' he called out, pointing his gun at them. 'The fight is over.'

Surprise at finding Clancy alive stopped both men in their tracks, fifty to sixty feet away.

'How the devil did you get out here?' Armstrong was dumbfounded.

'That's Clancy for you,' an oddly

familiar voice chimed in. 'He's got as many lives as a feral cat!'

'The posse is in the yard,' Clancy spoke again. 'You have no chance of getting away now.'

'You're out of bullets,' Armstrong sneered contemptuously. 'Even if they hang me, I'm going to gut shoot you and watch you die.'

The man lifted his gun to fire.

'No you don't,' Ringer warned him, turning his own gun on the man. 'The fight is over, boss. Killing Clancy won't change our fate.'

'You going soft on me? Now?' Armstrong demanded.

'We've played our cards and almost cleared the table, but we've lost this hand. It's over,' Ringer said. 'If Clancy is free, so are Tom and Kate. We can't kill them all before the posse catches us.'

Armstrong lowered his gun. 'You've been with me from the first, Ringer,' he said. 'I guess I can listen to you this one time.'

As soon as Ringer lowered his gun, Armstrong turned his pistol on him and pulled the trigger!

Ringer dropped his weapon and staggered backward from the bullet's impact.

Clancy, desperate to stop Armstrong from shooting again, fired at the ex-sergeant. The bullet must have missed, because the man swung quickly back around to face him.

Both of them fired again and again. When Clancy's hammer struck on an empty cartridge, the two of them were still both standing. For a long moment, they stared at one another.

Ringer had sunk to the ground, but Armstrong was still on his feet. He held his free hand over a wound to his chest and managed to stagger forward towards Clancy. His gun was still aimed in his direction and he trudged as if in deep snow.

'Damn your hide, Clancy,' Armstrong bellowed. 'You've ruined everything I had planned. If it's the last thing I do,

I'm going to see you dead.'

Clancy had barely noticed that a bullet had burned a path along his left arm, and there was a burning sensation from being grazed along his neck. Armstrong had come close, but he hadn't been able to hit Clancy square.

'Stop or die, Armstrong,' Clancy warned the man.

'You've spent your last rounds. I don't know how you managed nine shots, but I heard the click of your empty chamber. You're done.'

As the man paused and began to squeeze the trigger on his pistol, Clancy fired his round of grapeshot. It exploded against Armstrong's chest and knocked him off his feet. His pistol flew from his hand and he landed heavily on his back.

Clancy walked over to stand over the man. There was a shocked expression on Armstrong's face. Then he tried to laugh. 'Curse your hide . . . ' he rasped with his dying breath. 'You've got a gun . . . like . . . Wirz!'

Sergeant Fuller, also known as Fulton Armstrong, said nothing more. He was dead.

Clancy knelt down at Ringer's side. The man's eyes were open, but he had been mortally wounded. He didn't have long.

'Jeffrey,' Clancy said softly, able to recognize the man called Ringer, with the aid of the fire's light. 'I thought you were dead?'

His brother grimaced with pain, but managed to look up at him. 'I shamed our name, Morgan,' he muttered ruefully. 'I sold out the other prisoners so I could survive. It's why . . . ' He coughed and spat out a mouthful of blood. 'It's why I carved my name on that mass grave. I wanted you to believe that your brother had died in that filthy pesthole. I never wanted you to find out that I was a coward and a traitor.'

'You only did what you had to do to survive,' Clancy told him gently. 'I would have understood.'

But the boy's head rolled from side

203

to side. 'No . . . no, you . . . wouldn't.'

Clancy saw the life drain from Jeff's body. He gently removed the rawhide strap and the tarnished wedding ring that his brother wore around his neck, lowered his head and wept.

'Hey, Clancy!' York's voice shouted gleefully. 'We were afraid all of you had died inside the house! Did anyone else make it out alive?'

Clancy stood up as York and Darren came over to them. 'We're all safe,' he told them, blinking back his tears.

Darren announced, 'We've got three of them who will live long enough to stand trial.' They both peered at the two dead men on the ground.

'It appears you took care of Armstrong and Ringer. Wart's dead too.'

'Actually, Ringer had a change of heart. When you arrived with the posse, he tried to stop Armstrong from killing us.'

'You don't say,' York said. 'Well, that goes to show the man wasn't all bad.'

'No . . . he wasn't,' Clancy agreed.

Tom, Kate and Jenny all made their way up out of the wash. Clancy tipped his head in their direction.

'Jenny saved us from the fire. She also managed to get my gun so we could hold off Armstrong and his men until you got here.' He tucked the gun into his belt and shook hands with them both. 'You saved our lives arriving when you did.'

'That's what friends and neighbors do for each other,' York reflected.

'I was simply returning the favor,' Darren added with a grin. 'Remember, you saved me from being beaten to death.'

'The Freeman family could use some blankets. It's going to be a cold wait for morning.'

Darren hurried off to find what he could.

'Frosty York.' Tom addressed the liveryman as he made his way slowly over to them, 'You and the other farmers are a welcome sight indeed.'

'The farmers knew it was Armstrong

who was trying to drive them off their land, not you.'

'Armstrong was afraid someone would recognize him as Sergeant Fuller,' Clancy explained to Tom. 'The farmers all hail from his neck of the woods.'

York looked at the two gals, both hugging themselves with crossed arms, trying to keep from shivering.

'Let's go out front and see if we can round up those blankets. Once the fire goes out, it's gonna be a cool morning.'

* * *

It took the remainder of the night before the fire was completely extinguished. The freight wagon was loaded with the three dead and one wounded man. Then York took charge of the posse and prisoners. They headed down the trail toward town.

'Looks like you will have to move into a new house,' Clancy told Tom. 'Good thing Armstrong built one with lots of room.'

'Yes,' Tom agreed. 'I should think we'll be expanding soon. With you as my new foreman, I think we can make a go of the ranch.'

'It will help once we get a judge to award you the money from your stolen beef. You can pay off the mortgage and combine the two places into one.'

'I'm grateful to you, Clancy.' Tom was sincere. 'You've not only saved our ranch, you've helped to save our lives. I don't know if making you a foreman is enough to repay you for that.'

Clancy put his arm around Kate. Jenny moved in on his other side and held up a cat for him to see.

'This is Mittens,' she said. 'Shakes tried to save us, but one of the bad men kicked him. He was hiding out by the corral.'

'It was very brave of Shakes to try and protect you,' Clancy said. 'Think he and Mittens will like the new home?'

'Maybe, if Jenny likes it,' she said. Then, shyly, 'Are you coming too?'

'I'd like to,' Clancy replied. 'Would

that be all right with you?'

'Uh-huh,' she said quietly. 'And I think Kate would like it too.'

Clancy smiled at Kate and she laughed. 'Yes, I would like that very much. We are all going to be one big, happy family.'

THE END

We do hope that you have enjoyed reading this large print book.

Did you know that all of our titles are available for purchase?

We publish a wide range of high quality large print books including:
**Romances, Mysteries, Classics
General Fiction
Non Fiction and Westerns**

Special interest titles available in large print are:
**The Little Oxford Dictionary
Music Book, Song Book
Hymn Book, Service Book**

Also available from us courtesy of Oxford University Press:
**Young Readers' Dictionary
(large print edition)
Young Readers' Thesaurus
(large print edition)**

For further information or a free brochure, please contact us at:
**Ulverscroft Large Print Books Ltd.,
The Green, Bradgate Road, Anstey,
Leicester, LE7 7FU, England.
Tel:** (00 44) **0116 236 4325
Fax:** (00 44) **0116 234 0205**

THE HEAD HUNTERS

Mark Bannerman

Elmer Carrington, former Captain of the Texas Rangers, is the victim of a horrendous crime committed by the Mexican bandit, Mateo. Accompanied by Daniel Ramos, another victim, he sets off in pursuit of the man they hate. Travelling into Mexico, they encounter terrifying hazards, but nothing prepares them for the torture that awaits them when Carrington is given a hideous task. Failure to carry it out could mean death for them both . . .